THE

PARRSBORO

BOXING CLUB

BRUCE GRAHAM

POTTERSFIELD PRESS, LAWRENCETOWN BEACH, NOVA SCOTIA

Canadian Cataloguing in Publication Data

Graham, Bruce
    ISBN 1-895900-35-2
I. Title.
PS8563.R3143P37 2000   C813'.6   C00-950129-0
PR9199.3.G6732P37 2000

Edited by Julia Swan and Lesley Choyce

Cover photograph by Bruce Graham

Pottersfield Press gratefully acknowledges the ongoing support of the Nova Scotia Department of Tourism and Culture, Cultural Affairs Division as well as The Canada Council for the Arts. We acknowledge the financial support of the Government of Canada through the Book Publishing Industry Development Program for our publishing activities.

Pottersfield Press
83 Leslie Road
East Lawrencetown
Nova Scotia, Canada, B2Z 1P8
To order, phone toll-free 1-800-NIMBUS9 (1-800-646-2879)
Printed in Canada

THE CANADA COUNCIL | LE CONSEIL DES ARTS
FOR THE ARTS | DU CANADA
SINCE 1957 | DEPUIS 1957

NOVA SCOTIA
Tourism and Culture

Canadä

TO MALCOLM

It's a fairly big transition from writing for radio and television to writing a novel. In my own defense, I recognized this from the outset and knew I'd need a lot of help. I'm sure there are some people I'll miss in this acknowledgement and I hope they'll forgive me. However, some stand out as needing to be mentioned and specifically thanked for their unselfish assistance.

Author and playwright Lance Woolaver read early drafts and made many helpful suggestions in style and substance. Lance, thank you.

Once you're caught up in a writing project, you're not above asking close friends to cast a critical eye on your work. Tarah Schwartz and Liz Magnifico both made many positive contributions. Clarence Watson read an early draft and prevented me from falling into several grammatical glitches.

A special thank you to Lesley Choyce who saw something promising in my work. His encouragement and suggestions are greatly appreciated. The help of editor Julia Swan almost defies description. If I can use a boxing analogy, her defense and offence were solid. She stopped me from straying, kept refining the details and jabbed away at the redundant and superfluous. Julia, from Duff, Jean, Curly, Mouse and the other characters in *The Parrsboro Boxing Club*, thank you for making us more human.

Finally, my most heartfelt thanks goes to Helen Wasson who read and proofed the final drafts of this book, making valuable contributions not only to style, but about the town we love in the era when we were young. Helen's contributions go beyond words.

THE

PARRSBORO BOXING CLUB

If you could look down from a great mountain on Parrsboro you would see the salt water snaking its way for a mile from the Minas Basin to the center of the town. You would see the one main street — the commercial district — where on Saturday nights the stores stay open until nine-thirty and folks shop for Sunday dinner. Standing on that mountain you could see the steeples of four churches and plenty of white houses partially obscured by maple trees. The town of two thousand is surrounded by the Cobequid Mountains, a low range of wooded hills. White and yellow birch and maple trees mingle with evergreens in these hills and small brooks pour over steep ravines, turning into waterfalls. In midair their falling water can catch the sun's rays, producing tiny rainbows just before the water splashes into pools and changes back to a brook rushing along the forest floor, always moving towards the sea.

Parrsboro is one of the five lean towns of Cumberland County. Of these towns Springhill is the best known because of its misfortunes. Twice in the 1950s Springhill was the focus of world attention when its coal mines rocked and bumped. People from all over the county came to Springhill. They came into town, driving past the union hall and the houses coated with coal dust, to stand and wait by the mouth of the pit. They waited in the rain sometimes and in bleak chilly mornings as the Salvation Army served coffee. Day after day they'd come and wait to see if the miners would get out alive. Some did. Many didn't.

Twenty-eight miles away our town's industry had already disappeared by the time of Springhill's sorrows. Parrsboro still had its bragging rights, something no other community could claim, the highest rise and fall of tides in the world. In the morning boats are riding high in the water. A few hours later those same boats are sitting on the sea bottom, their keels kissing the gritty sand. Twice a day the tide reaches its high water mark and twice a day the lighthouse is surrounded by miles of mud flats. The water has disappeared. What has also disappeared are the ships that once made our little town a maritime trading center. Beautiful barks and brigs, and later two- and three-masted schooners, once dotted our horizon, their billowing sails a monument to the capitalism that carried Nova Scotia coal and lumber all over the world.

It was in Parrsboro my father started his boxing club. He said it was a chance for young men to learn pugilistic skills: the art of the bob and weave, the jab, the hook, the counterpunch and, most important of all, footwork. Over the years the club attracted many of the town's young men. Most dropped out, unable to take the training and my father's verbal barrage. In his eyes you were either committed or you were wasting his time. The pressure was extreme, the practice long, the training hard. Twice a week there was sparring and on Saturday there was roadwork, starting with a slow run around the town's perimeter, known as the four-mile square.

He usually ran with us even though he had a bad leg. Many a citizen of Parrsboro would unexpectedly come upon this strange parade of steamy adolescents led by a limping man whose disability forced him to leap slightly upward at every step, as if he were trying to snatch something out of the air in front of him. He was usually unshaven, white stubble on his beet-red face. As we ran he offered no pep talk, no calls of encouragement. The only sound was our hard breath mingled with almost inaudible sighs and wheezes in the hurtful sucking of hot air. Some couldn't go on and staggered to the side of the road. There were sprained ankles and a broken leg when an exhausted Baxter Hebb fell into a ditch.

Parents complained and took their children out of the club. But a few remained. Hard core and hard driven, they survived the roadwork and sparring and my father's harangues. I don't really think my father cared if anyone stayed in the club as long as I was there. The club was really his way of making sure I was ready.

Given our training it wasn't surprising in competitions the Parrsboro Boxing Club did well. The club got mentioned in the sports pages of the Halifax and Moncton newspapers. Even critics of Alex Martin grudgingly admitted the boxing club gave the town a certain renown.

My mother cared nothing for the town's renown. In a heated argument her voice would never get as loud as his but it had a painful sob to it as she accused him of torturing me. In a way I guess she was right but I'd rather endure the torture and win my father's approval. I never complained. Complaining would bring on more hostility, and seeing them argue and hearing my mother's sobs was hurtful.

My boxing career began early. Not only was I exposed to the roadwork and sparring, but I'd box with my father every day until my mother would force a temporary stop to my training. These lapses never lasted long and within a day or two I'd be back at the punching bag or boxing with him in the homemade ring in our basement. Once my mother was so adamant she threatened to leave him and take me with her. That stopped my training for two whole weeks. I was eight years old.

I

Parrsboro

Nova Scotia

It isn't out of disrespect I call my father "the old man." It's something we do in this part of the world. Your father is the old man and your mother is "the old woman." My mother detested the term and would never permit its use. So she is called Mother but my father is my old man. Dewey calls his father Lloyd as if they're brothers. It wouldn't work with us. I couldn't call him Alex; Duff and Alex just wouldn't be normal. It isn't just me. All the members of the boxing club call him "the old man." When he's happy with us we're "his boys." When he's not happy he calls us the world's dumbest children, idiots, knuckleheads and assholes. As trainer, manager and master of the Parrsboro Boxing Club, the old man organizes events, promotes the club, raises the money and bullies the boxers.

My old man is what you might call a dynamo, a boxing fanatic. When I was born he wanted to call me Rocky. Rocky Robinson Martin. My mother would have none of it. No Rocky, under any circumstances. He had the papers signed; she had them unsigned. It was a deadlock. Finally he relented and Rocky became Robert. She said it was a compromise anyway since she had already agreed to my second name — Robinson. It's after Sugar Ray, the fighter most admired by my old man.

When I was born, he tried to make Rocky stick as a nickname. Called me Rocky the first three years of my life and encouraged others to do the same. It didn't work. Everybody calls me Duff. There have been family arguments over how Duff originated. My cousin Doris says she started calling me that when I was a baby, but nobody believes her. The old man says Doris wouldn't know the truth if she spent the night with it.

The old man perfected his boxing in the navy and became Canadian military champ. He was headed for a pro career as a middleweight when Curtis Gillis dropped his shotgun as they were duck hunting. Part of the shot ripped the old man's leg to shreds, giving him a permanent limp and a new career as a hardware merchant.

The Parrsboro Boxing Club has its home in St. Bridget's church hall. It may be the only church hall where the walls are lined with photographs of boxers. You are encouraged to look at them but not to touch them. How they got there gives you some idea of what kind of guy the old man is when it comes to boxing. His ship is tied up in New York City. He hears Joe Louis is sparring in town, getting ready for a fight. The old man buys a camera, walks all day, finds the gym, blusters his way past some very tough looking people. He's in uniform — Canadian Navy. Then he gets Joe Louis, one of the shyest men on the face of the earth, to pose with him. Honest to God. The Brown Bomber decorates the walls of the Parrsboro Boxing Club. Back on ship, the old man takes his petty officer a really good bottle of rum, swaps bridge duty and is back the next day with more film to take pictures of Joe Louis sparring. He's the only photographer there, the only one allowed in. The best of these photographs hang in our house, the next best are on the walls of the club where they're part of the initiation for every young boxer.

"Look at the legs," he says. "More muscles in the legs than the arms. You know why?"

They never do.

"Because the legs are more important. Legs give you leverage, and leverage gives you power."

Everybody goes through it, even visitors. The "look at the legs" speech, the "how he met Joe Louis" speech. He is nothing if not consistent, says my mother.

My mother is different in every way. A school teacher who reads books, not the sports pages. She practices building my vocabulary while he builds my biceps. She calls the old man "bombastic" and I like that word. She pretty well lets him run things until he gets out of hand, about once or twice a week. Then she stands her ground.

"Oh no, you won't. The boy has had enough, Alex, and I've had enough too. That's all the training for tonight, and tomorrow I want him out with his friends, not cooped up in that basement. You're going to ruin his health."

"Ruin nothing! You know any other kid that's developed like that? Ruin his health? I'm making him strong."

"A child's development is more than muscles, Alex. If you ever read anything but the sports pages you might know children need time with their friends, in the fresh air."

"For God's sake, Jean! He has plenty of fresh air. He runs every day, doesn't he?"

Then she reverts to her ultimate weapon, a book on child development written by some doctor somewhere. Whenever she opens it to read him something, he disappears. That book is like a Buck Rogers laser gun. It can make the old man vanish. When he goes out the door or down the stairs, there is a faint look of satisfaction on her face. Another victory in the middle rounds of life. She sometimes smiles at me then and slightly nods her head as if to say brains beat brawn anytime. Underneath her bookish manners she's as tough as him but she doesn't waste her interventions. She only risks his rebuke when he's really been rough, riding me hard over my hook or criticizing counterpunching or the weaknesses or my stance, which he thinks is too far forward. She'll rescue me and he'll either explode or just grumble and back off, giving me some breathing room. Then he's back with new intensity.

He taught me everything about boxing. With the old man it's hours in the ring in our basement. "Keep the elbows in," he'll growl, then a minute or two later, as we circle each other, there will be a question dripping in criticism. "What are you doin' with that right? Come on. For God's sake, use it. Come on! Come on!" Then it's praise, short jabs of it. "Good! Good! Good!" as I fire rights and lefts at him. Sometimes my frustration gets the better of me. One night I lunge at him, trying for a body blow. He's too fast and, I think, expecting it. I'm off balance and a rapid tap to the side of the head sprawls me on the mat.

"Getting mad is the stupidest thing a fighter can do." He steps through the ropes and is gone upstairs and I'm still face down on the canvas, knowing he's right. Again.

With my mother, it's words and books at the kitchen table. A chapter of Robert Louis Stevenson's *Treasure Island* is read to me each evening before bed. She even reads me poems: Yeats, Tennyson and Robert Browning. One evening while I'm having a cup of warm chocolate she is reading me one of her favorites, George Meredith's *Love in the Valley*. The old man is having a beer, reading *Ring* magazine. She pretends he isn't there.

"Such a look will tell that the violets are peeping,
Coming the rose: and unaware a cry."

"Aw Jesus, Jean." He gets up with a snort. "What kind of crap ya puttin' in that boy's head?"

She doesn't stop.

"Springs in her bosom for odours and for color,
Covert and the nightingale; she knows not why."

I never see my parents as a couple but as separate parts. *Her world.* The kitchen world of words, cookies and kindness. *His world.* The basement world of boxing, of praise, pushing and pain. I live in both worlds and extract what I can from them. I don't like it when he pushes me but I'm not crazy about the poetry either. Yet I seldom complain. Living in both worlds keeps them from colliding.

She plays bridge and drinks tea. He plays pool and drinks beer. A couple of times a year they might go to the movies together. "I'm not goin' to any of the Mitzy Gaynor dancing stuff," he'll say.

"Well, don't expect me to go to that awful war movie," she'll reply.

Once in a while there is something at the Gem theater they can agree on. After the dishes are done, they'll put their hats and coats on and go out the door. When I was old enough to be left alone I'd wait

11

for the Studebaker to pull out of the driveway, then I'd sit in the big rocking chair in the kitchen. I'd just listen to the stillness of the empty house. I am an only child but seldom alone. But when I am, I like it.

It's not that my parents can't be nice to each other. Despite such different personalities, at times they laugh. My mother is a good cook and my father enjoys her food. They even joke about the youthful absurdity of their romance and marriage.

"He swept me off my feet" is how she puts it. "I was a young school teacher from Bass River and along comes this handsome sailor with his smile and his swagger." A small pain passes her eyes as she remembers his walk before the accident. They had only been married a month when he almost lost his leg. At the hospital, they picked shotgun pellets out of his bloody flesh and told her they might have to amputate. She refused to let them. It's the bond that makes their life together bearable. He always thanked her for that. With the tenacity of a bulldog, he defied the doctors. He worked like a madman and, after fifteen months, could walk again. His boxing career and his military career were gone. So was the swagger.

2

S NOOKY AND F EAR

There has been a lot of pain lately. We're getting ready for the annual bouts in Moncton. Turning sixteen ten days ago means this is my first appearance before hundreds of people. Wednesday is my coming out. Is that what they call it? After years of sitting with our parents, my best friend Dewey and I are in the ring, the old man in our corner, the hundred or so Parrsboro fans drowned out by partisan New Brunswickers. There are eleven members in the Parrsboro Boxing Club, aged ten to nineteen. The seven of us sixteen and over will be boxing in Moncton. Of the seven, two have never been to the fights in Moncton and have yet to really understand what intense noise does to your nerves.

Moncton is a small city, forty times bigger than Parrsboro with more talent to draw from, and they draw from far and wide, all the way to New Brunswick's north shore — Acadian boys, tough as nails. The old man says it's illegal since they live miles from Moncton. He's protested, but to no avail. With its collection of boxers, Moncton wins most of the bouts. Most but not all.

Last year Dickey Camcron was in a real brawl. A big kid named Gaeton Leblanc put a swelling under his eye. Dickey was in the third and final round, behind on points. Gaeton had given him a slight nosebleed. For all the old man's lecturing about the jab, Dickey needed a big power punch. Knockouts almost never happen in our boxing but Dickey let fly with a right hook that hit Gaeton on the jaw with a "whap" you could hear all over the arena. Gaeton dropped — deadweight.

Two bouts later Woody Wright won a split decision. Aside from those wins, there was another very close decision in Moncton's favor, three more Moncton victories and one draw where we were clearly robbed and where the old man almost lost it. I thought the crowd was going to kill him. Moncton fight fans take special pleasure in booing my old man. We left that night with two wins, a draw and four losses. No matter. The school bus taking us home was filled with the sense of victory. Dickey had thrown the punch of the night and everyone who knew boxing, knew it.

I'm hoping all the noise in Moncton doesn't make me nervous. My biggest crowd was a hundred and fifty at the Port Greville church picnic. It was last summer and the scariest fight of my life, three rounds with Snooky Redden that I came close to losing. Lawrence, my biggest critic, insists I did lose but they were scared to give it to Snooky because they thought the old man might go berserk. He almost went berserk anyway, running up and down outside of the ring, yelling and shouting in front of the church. My mother gave him an earful that night and told him she'd never been so humiliated.

I'll never forget that Sunday afternoon. The church lawn was loaded with tables of fried chicken, baked beans and apple pie. There were foot races and a pony ride and music by the Parrsboro Citizens Band. Right in the middle of the lawn stood a regulation ring.

No one ever wants to fight Snooky because of what they call his "other" weapon. Snooky drools. There is always a stream running down his chin. You give him a good jab and the drool splatters back at you. He drools in the winter too and it freezes on his coat and Snooky faces unkind comments. "Here comes old frozen coat," they'll chime on the way to school. "If Canada ever runs out of water we'll just put a spout in Snooky Redden's head."

Drool or no drool, Snooky is a good boxer. He comes at me quickly, gets in a good left in the first seconds of the first round. Then a shower of jabs and another hook. My face is smarting. I can feel the beginning of fear, and tears dance at the back of my eyes.

The fear is not of losing, although that would be bad enough. No, it's not of losing, it's of crying. I'd rather have him kill me than start to cry. I couldn't handle the shame. Not with the girls there, sitting on their blankets, in their Sunday clothes, overdressed for a picnic but not planning to run any relay races. Girls I'm in school with, sitting by the ring watching, sixteen-, seventeen-year-olds, including the enormously good-looking Heather Harrington. I'd rather die than cry.

I've heard of young fighters so scared or nervous their bowels let go right in the ring. Can you imagine? Tears in your eyes, shorts full of shit. There wouldn't be a hole deep enough to crawl into. Thoughts of tears, fear and shit help me recover. I have a better second round and get in some good licks in the third, including a punch that staggers Snooky, the drool splattering over me. People cheer at the end. Judges' decision — a draw.

That was a year ago. I've gained sixteen pounds and a lot of punching power since then. I work a heavier bag, spar with bigger guys, and run four miles a day in heavy army boots to build my legs. Legs are important.

My opponent Wednesday is an Irish kid from Moncton by the name of Jack Ryan. I wonder what he's doing at this very minute. A shiver runs through me as I picture him in a gym, working a heavy bag, covered in sweat.

3

LAWRENCE AND DEWEY

As well as being my best friend, Dewey Hunter is the smartest person I know. My mother says he has both intense and intelligent eyes. Dewey reads a lot and knows a lot of things. He is the best student with the highest marks. It is only in boxing where I can do better than him.

The old man says Dewey would be a better boxer if he could keep his head up. You can get tired or careless, even with all that excitement running through you. Dewey will often drop his head when he's tired in the final round. In five-round bouts Dewey has a problem.

Danny Yorke on the other hand is a very average student with a very good right hand. We're all considered middleweights, 140 to 150 pounds. Danny is fast and usually very effective, but his last fight three months ago in Amherst was a disaster. He lost and lost badly. I'm not convinced his heart is in boxing. I know he is nervous about Moncton.

The old man says if he got that mass of sandy hair out of his eyes he might be able to see something. Danny is a handsome kind of guy, attractive to girls. He's usually a smooth talker while Dewey is a smooth thinker. Me, I'm not smooth but I do have a left hook and a right jab. Other than boxing I'm very average.

Aside from boxing, the one burning passion in my life is the sea. I love being on the water. That's where Lawrence comes into my life. He operates the *Fundy Mist*, one of Dewey's father's boats. Lawrence is ten years older than me and I go fishing with him whenever I can, even though it means a lot of barbs and critical comments. Yesterday we were moving lobster traps down the basin. He spits tobacco with purpose over the side in a straight shot — a sure sign he's going to say something. I know he's going to talk about Moncton.

"So you're fighting that Irish kid, eh? You'll get your ass kicked." I wipe a little juice off my face. With Lawrence you can't avoid the spray; his checkered shirt carries full notification he is a chewer, a man who works with grease and fish. After a day with Lawrence I find similar stains on my clothes. Lawrence waits for my answer. He wants an argument. He likes to put me on the defensive, to needle me. I complained once to Dewey about Lawrence and his shitty attitude. Dewey says Lawrence has never had a woman and that's why he's so grumpy.

"We've never had a woman either, Dew."

"It's different when you get in your twenties. If you're that old and have never had it, you get all bound up."

So Lawrence is bound up badly. But I suffer his insults and digs because he has a boat and he fishes and lets me help and even occasionally pays me. I really don't care about the money. It's being on the water that counts.

I live in a different world on the water. As you come into Parrsboro, the town can look like one of those toy towns — the kind you buy in the Eaton's catalogue and arrange the buildings on the floor. The only difference is Parrsboro has something those toy towns don't have — the old wharves. Not really wharves anymore, just rotting timbers now, bleached white, peeled and eaten; pillars of Parrsboro's prime when tern schooners, barkentines and brigantines tied up to them. Wooden ships, built along this shore carried lumber, coal, and general cargo all over the world. By the 1920s steam and steel had replaced sail and wood and the beautiful ships disappeared, leaving Parrsboro's wharves idle, its harbor empty.

Parrsboro is on the Minas Basin on the east coast of Canada. Between Nova Scotia and New Brunswick, the mighty Bay of Fundy splits into two prongs — the basin and the bay. The Minas Basin stretches miles inland past the rocky cliffs and rolling hills of Nova Scotia's Cumberland and Colchester Counties. The other prong, Chignecto Bay, slices into the less rugged terrain and redder soil of New Brunswick's Albert County. Parrsboro has the world's highest tides. It's a place with history and it's on the water that I can somehow be part of a past I wish I'd lived in, been part of, and totally missed.

Mouse Morrison comes fishing with us sometimes. Lawrence gives Mouse an even harder time than he gives me. At nineteen Mouse is the oldest member of the boxing club. He is also the old man's biggest problem. After months of intensive training, Mouse has fallen back into his old ways. He's refusing to bob and weave. Instead he stands flat-footed in the middle of the ring, one arm extended like a traffic cop. Mouse relies on his only asset, brute strength. He doesn't have style or grace, just power. My mother says Mouse is so awkward his opponents lose by laughing themselves silly. Mouse can look awkward. He may throw forty punches and miss forty times but when he finally connects — wow.

The old man has been working with Mouse for months, trying to give him a defensive position and some counterpunching ability. It hasn't worked. Mouse doesn't even look like a fighter and the old man is afraid he and Mouse will be laughed out of Moncton Wednesday night.

The one person in the club the old man isn't worried about is me. He knows I'm ready. Don't call me cocky, but I've learned the art of the dodge and duck. I've been brought up in the school of the bob and weave. It's so much a part of me, not only do I use it in the ring but I've extended it to life itself. I bob around high school assignments and dodge another hour of sparring. I bob and weave past the old man when he's distracted. When he's working with Mouse is the best time to scram. He's so busy he doesn't catch on. I wait until he's screaming at Mouse then I duck out the door and slip off the premises to find Lawrence and the *Fundy Mist*.

The old bob and weave has worked again.

4

D EWEY'S F IGHT

The old man doesn't want us hanging around before the fights so we arrived with less than an hour before the first bout. This drives the Moncton organizers wild, but after fifteen years they're used to my old man.

There are twenty-four people on the school bus that brings us to Moncton — fighters, trainers and fans. Other people drive the hour and fifteen minutes to cheer on the local boys.

Compared to Parrsboro, Moncton is big time with a dressing room for every two or three fighters. They have showers, a sink and even a mirror.

Dewey and Danny go with me. The bouts start with the sixteen-year-olds and continue on to the older guys. The three of us are the youngest and we're first: Dewey against a kid named Norman Boudreau, Danny on the second card, then me. Then there are the seventeen-year-olds: Marcus Chambers and Curtis Blenkhorn. Next the eighteen-year-olds and Plucky Wagstaff and Mouse with the resisting left.

We change into our shorts. There isn't much talking. We tape each other's hands while the old man and his assistant, Curly Dickie, work with the older guys. The bob and weave gets a good workout.

We shadowbox constantly — three sixteen-year-olds filled with nervous energy.

Ten minutes before the first bout, the old man comes in to give us the pep talk. He's so concentrated on boxing the roof could fall in and he wouldn't notice. At times like this there is a fierceness in his eyes that's almost scary. He's preoccupied with stance, footwork, guard-up and jab.

"Jesus, boys, keep those jabs going. Don't stand there like a brick shithouse waiting to be hit!" Alone with me his pep talks are much different. He'll almost ramble and I feel I'm listening in on his soliloquy about courage and the quality of a man. Standing next to me he'll put his hand on my shoulder but he's off somewhere. I know this sounds silly, but it's kind of, well, it's okay, him doing that. Other guys might be embarrassed, and I guess I would be if anyone saw us but it's in those minutes I love my old man best.

Tonight it's the routine. General pep talk for all of us, and he pays me no special attention. He doesn't have to. I know tonight is different. I'm going in the ring in front of hundreds of people and I know he's proud of me.

The old man leaves again and the minutes tick by. The noise outside is louder now as people fill the seats. There's coughing and yelling and spitting and doors slamming and many feet pounding on the old wooden floor. The Moncton arena holds fifteen hundred and these fights usually draw close to a full house. We are the first attraction. There are always a couple of professional fights to guarantee a crowd.

The noise can be incredible. We hear it now, the sound building like a throbbing engine, gathering steam, gaining momentum, getting a life of its own. Noise can overtake everything. It can rattle a fighter, particularly a young fighter whose experience is limited to church picnics and barbecues sponsored by the Oddfellows Lodge or the Legion. It helps me that I've come to Moncton all these years, sitting in the crowd, being part of the clamor of fifteen hundred zealous fight fans.

"This is going to be a full house," Curly says. The racket is already ricocheting off the old wooden walls. The old man is back, giving Dewey information he'd picked up about Norman Boudreau. The book on Boudreau is he's not much of a puncher but has endurance and can stay on his feet. "So play it safe, box well and remember," says the old man looking particularly at Dewey, "keep your head up."

Dew's habit of letting his head drop a bit makes him an easier target. We're all nervous. Our parents are in the audience. "I hate going first," Dew says to himself as he bobs and fires a left and a right at the scarred and grimy wall.

The public address system comes on with a crackle and the crowd roars. "Good luck, Dewey," Danny and I chime as he leaves the dressing room with the old man and Curly. He gives us a big smile and the gloves-up sign. The crowd is getting to its feet. They're playing "O Canada."

The old man has his rules and one of them is you don't watch any fight until yours is over. He is a stickler about rules. The reason for this one is simple; it can throw off your concentration and concentration is a fighter's biggest asset next to footwork. Danny and I open the dressing room door anyway and sneak down the corridor for a peek. We can't see anything but steps, bleachers and feet. We would have to walk up eight steps to be able to look down the aisle to the ring and the old man might see us.

The ring announcer is talking. "For many years the Parrsboro Boxing Club has brought its best to Moncton and we're happy to see the tradition continue. Please give a spirited Moncton welcome to our first Parrsboro fighter, sixteen-year-old Dewey Hunter." A huge ovation goes up and even bigger applause for Norman Boudreau. Danny and I listen at the end of the corridor as the bell rings and the fight begins.

Within seconds something happens. We can tell by the noise. One fighter has scored a good punch. Hope it's Dewey. Come on, buddy. There is another roar and I have an uneasy feeling. There is too much enthusiasm, too many cheers by an overwhelmingly — what's the word? — "partisan" crowd. We walk back as the bell signals the end of round one. We stay by the open door of the dressing room. Danny is looking a little pale.

In round two, first cheers then silence. Then a slight shudder through the crowd followed by wild cheering and another roar like thunder that startles both of us. "Jesus!" says Danny. "What was that?"

There is a small knot in my stomach — an uneasy feeling my best friend is not doing well. A second later Curly flies through the doorway and grabs the towels and the old man's first aid kit. He is white.

5

PUKING AND PUNCHING

He rushes out without answering our questions. There is pandemonium outside. I can't stand it. I run out with Danny following me. We race to the top of the stairs; the ring is four hundred feet away. It's filled with people, including my old man, Dewey's father, the police, the referee, and guys from the St. John's Ambulance.

My old man and Dewey's father are kneeling over Dewey, who is lying on his back, his eyes closed. His father is holding his head while one of the St. John Ambulance men gives him smelling salts. Dewey is beginning to cough and move his head.

"Alex, you should have stopped the fight after the first round," Dewey's father yells, and glares at the old man. "That kid was too big for Dewey. What the hell's wrong with you?"

Still bending over my defeated and semi-conscious friend, my old man looks at Dewey and declares he'll be all right. Then, looking at Lloyd Hunter with grit in his eye, the old man says, "If he'd done what I told him, he wouldn't have been open for that left."

"Bullshit," roars Lloyd.

I'm ten feet away and despite the chaos I can hear every word they're saying, including the policeman who says, "Gentlemen, please. We want to take him to the hospital."

Lloyd Hunter looks at my old man. "That's it, Alex, he's not fighting anymore."

"Gentlemen, please." The policeman moves over to Dewey. "We want to move him."

The old man's face is beet-red, and when he sees Danny and me standing there he snarls, "Get back to the dressing room." Away we fly.

Back in the dressing room Danny moans, "God Almighty. Dewey's going to quit the club. Jesus, I hope he's all right." Danny is flushed and white at the same time. His cheeks and neck are rosy and his forehead, underneath the mass of sandy, unruly, curly hair is snow white. He's breathing hard and looking ill. "I've never seen anyone knocked out before," he says as he slumps against the wall and slowly sinks to his knees. Then suddenly he vomits over his shorts and robe and the floor. I look at him, trying to think if there is something I should do.

God, what a mess. The night is turning out to be awful. In less than ten minutes Dewey has been knocked out and Danny is puking all over the place. Curly and the old man come through the door together. They look at Danny. "Oh God," cries Curly. "Oh shit," cries the old man. Curly gets Danny into the washroom.

The old man stands in front of me. It's one of those moments you realize your father is aging, getting old so slightly you hardly notice until you really look. Under the harsh lights of the changing room he's haggard and I feel a whole lot of things right now for my father. He's sweating and stares back at me with his hands on his hips, his face flushed, white hair askew. He has this habit of taking his middle finger and pushing his glasses up on his nose. He does it now.

"This evening isn't turning out so hot for us. You're going to have to fight next."

"How's Dewey?" I ask.

"He'll be fine. They just took him to the hospital to check him over."

"His dad is mad at you, isn't he?"

"Never mind that. Get ready. You're going to have to go next. Can't have Danny facing a fighter in his condition." He turns and leaves me there. I can hear Danny hurling in the bathroom.

Curly comes out. "Get your gloves on, kid."

As he is doing up my gloves I ask, "What happened?"

Curly shrugs. "Dewey took a hard left in the first round. This kid isn't supposed to be much of a puncher but he hit Dewey like a kick from a horse, twice in the first round, and Dewey was a little woozy. Maybe the ref should have stopped the fight but he didn't. Maybe your old man should have thrown in the towel but he didn't." He ties my gloves tightly.

The old man is back. "Come on, kid, let's go. They're waiting." And away we go, me in silver boxing shorts with a black stripe down the sides, wearing one of the two white terry cloth robes with Parrsboro Boxing Club on the back. The old man is on one side of me, Curly on the other. We march down the center aisle as the crowd, now worked up, hoots, boos, hisses and cheers.

6

FACING JACK RYAN

The smoke and noise are overpowering. Marching down the aisle, the boos and cheers rise in a collective chorus. Clouds of tobacco smoke hang over the ring. I don't look at the crowd as we move along. "Always keep your eyes straight ahead" is the old man's instruction and I follow it. Jack Ryan and his handlers are entering the ring at the same time so the boos for me turn to cheers for him.

Ryan glares at me during the ref's instructions. Part of landing the first blow on your opponent is to beat him with your eyes. I'm afraid Ryan notices me wince as our eyes first make contact. I want to make up for that, show him I'm not bothered by him on any level. I don't have my mouthpiece in yet, so as we touch gloves, after the ref's instructions, I say in a loud voice, "Jack, your fly is open." For a tiny instant, a split second, nervous eyes flicker towards his crotch. I consider the non-fighting part of the fight a draw.

The old man is by my left ear. "Keep your feet moving and let's see what he's got right off the start." I know his meaning. Hit him hard early. He won't be expecting it and it will make him cautious.

The bell rings and I'm away, into my first big fight. I dance up to Ryan and get in a couple of right jabs; he doesn't respond. He looks tight, nervous. Strangely, for all that's happened tonight, I feel remarkably loose. He tries a jab, it falls short. I move in and let go a couple more jabs, bob and throw two more. The second two land on the side of his face. Of six jabs, I've landed four, two of them good ones. Ryan is a red-headed guy with a light complexion and his face is already turning pink. His manager is yelling something at him, when he lunges trying for a left hook. Swoosh — I feel the air from his haymaker. The swing leaves him slightly off balance and open. I hit him hard, with a right hook — my best punch. He sways but stays on his feet.

The bell ends round one.

As I walk to my corner, Curly is smiling.

"Okay," the old man says, "don't get cocky just cause ya took the first one."

"Ya shook 'em good, but don't get cocky," Curly repeats.

I can never imagine under what circumstances I am allowed to get cocky. If I won the world title, the old man would be there telling me not to get cocky.

Round two.

Ryan changes his stance, now leading with his left. He lets go a couple of insincere jabs. I hit him again with a left hook as the old man screams, "Jab. Come on. Jab." But the hook finds its mark. He counters with a right to my stomach. It hurts. As I back away, he tries the same punch. Foolish choice; even with my guard down I'm too far away. His second attempt at a body blow leaves his face unguarded. He tries again. This time I work my feet in and hit him, hard, with another left hook. He is a good counterpuncher and hits me on the side of my face. "Footwork," I can hear the old man over the roar of the crowd. I move away, rotate on my toes and come in on him with a flurry of left jabs. He shatters my attack with a straight right cross that sends a thousand pinpricks through my left shoulder. The bell rings.

No one is smiling in my corner now. The old man can drive me crazy at times, but when it comes to sizing up a fighter no one can do it better. He's back at my left ear. "Listen, kid, this guy drops his shoulder every time he fires his right. Counterpunch with your right next time."

"You got his face nice and rosy," says Curly as the bell rings.

Round three.

He comes at me like a man possessed. This happens when a young fighter loses the first round and wins the second. He's tasted success and wants it to continue. The old man has told me it's always a dangerous time for the fighter with a small lead. Your opponent gets a little reckless. If he lands one good punch your lead evaporates. I let him flail away. He isn't touching me, but his motion gets the crowd going and that gets him going. "Watch!" I can hear the old man yell at the top of his voice. "Watch!"

Ryan continues to flail away with jabs, then he tries a right, and sure enough his shoulder drops, leaving his head exposed. The next time he does that I'm in. I rotate my feet, getting ready to throw a hook. So far, in round three he's thrown about fifteen punches, two hitting me with glancing blows. I've thrown one left. As the old man often says, the numbers matter. But what matters more is where they're going. Of course it's true you've got to throw punches to look like you're in the fight. The round is wearing down and I'm anxious. He throws a right cross that goes over my shoulder and his shoulder drops. This is it. This might be my only good punch in the final round. I fire my right hook with all the power I can muster, putting the leverage in my legs. The punch catches him square on the chin and his feet fly right off the canvas. He is almost in a sitting position as he drops.

The crowd is in an uproar. Knockouts with nineteen- or twenty-year-old fighters are rare but with sixteen-year-olds, they never happen. Jack Ryan is twitching now, coming around from the smelling salts. The Parrsboro fans are going crazy, cheering and yelling, "Duff, Duff, Duff!"

The old man looks at me and smiles.

7

H O M E T O W N   H E R O

News of the Moncton knockouts spread like wildfire. The entire fight card is swirling in controversy. Sixteen-year-old boys knocking each other out! What's the meaning of this! In an editorial, the *Moncton Times* asks why young people are being taught to hurt each other. The lack of headgear also becomes an issue. It's raised by a member of the legislature and the New Brunswick government promises to investigate. There are letters to the editors. Dewey's father isn't helping. He publicly criticizes the boxing program and the old man. As Lawrence says, "The fur is flying."

The old man works an entire week drawing up a rebuttal. Page after page on the benefits of boxing and how it teaches young men skills they can carry through life. He quotes sports writers, fighters and commentators. His habit of saving every article on boxing is now paying off. The paper tells him it's too long for a letter to the editor, but they find it worthy and run most of it on the editorial page.

My parents handle the controversy differently. My mother is embarrassed. The old man doesn't say it but he is stung. He doesn't shut down the boxing club for the rest of the summer, but comes very close. We spar only once or twice a week. Saturday sparring sessions are cancelled. The old man is preoccupied and unusually quiet. Curly is often at our house now and they talk in low voices over beer at the kitchen table.

All the criticism isn't coming from the outside. There is plenty coming from my mother. She says he should have stopped Dewey's fight after the first round. She tells him he is the world's most stubborn man and that Curly is a simple-minded moron. She says the old man only puts up with him because Curly agrees with everything the old man says.

"Shows he's smarter than some people" is his only reply.

"You live in a dream world, Alex, and common sense and good judgment are not allowed in."

Moncton has caused a widening gulf between my parents. Twice in the last week I've caught my mother crying, her tears falling into the soapy water as she's over the sink with the supper dishes. When I put my arms around her she tells me she expects more of me than to be someone who hurts people.

"Yet that's exactly what he's taught you."

Quiet talks between them take place when I'm out of the room but these usually end with the old man erupting, his voice shaking the dishes in the china cabinet. "I've worked damn hard to make him a fighter and now you want us to stop? You want to raise a sissy, a man who can't look after himself." He's snarling and she's raising her voice.

"I want to raise a man who respects, not hurts, other people. As usual, Alex, you've gone too far, you've taken that boy's youth away from him. Let him live his own life, not one you can't live."

It goes on like that. Both of them try to make me their ally but I can't take sides. I can't because I really don't know. I love boxing, love my father, love my mother, love her books mostly, and her words for sure. How do I choose between them?

The tension drives me out of the house for endless hours along the shore. I spend my time skipping rocks on the water. If you hit the water just right with a flat, round stone it will bounce several times on the surface before sinking. I've become an expert. Twenty-two is my highest number. The distance between skips getting shorter and shorter until the rock kisses the surface a final time and disappears, its dance concluded.

Things are just as strained at Dewey's house. He's embarrassed by Moncton but more embarrassed his father won't let him box. They've had fierce arguments.

"I want to get back in the ring. This is shitty being forced to quit by your father. The rest of my life I'll be the kid who got beaten then protected by his daddy." He says bitterly, "I wish the bastard had killed me."

It's unsettling when Dewey adds that I'm lucky to have a father who supports me. "Yes," I say. "He does."

As a way of patching things up between them, Lloyd gives Dewey a little catboat for his seventeenth birthday. It's five years old with a center sail. It's in this little boat that we master the art of sailing. We pack a lunch each day and sail for hours. Up the basin to Five Islands, then over to Cape Blomidon and Hantsport. We have to wait hours sometimes for the tide to turn, since the harbor is dry twice a day. We bob up and down while hand lining for flounder and cod. The heavy cod line has two lead weights that quickly sink into forty feet of water.

We discuss every subject but boxing. I've known Dewey since grade four but during these days we share secrets we've never talked about. I can put the topics into a few categories — our parents, our futures, school, girls, sex, movies, sex, sports, sex, fishing, sex. We make a list of the top ten women in the world we would most like to bed. Movie star Jane Russell is my first choice, a big-breasted, full-figured woman. Dewey's pick is totally opposite, toothpick-thin Audrey Hepburn, more meat on a hockey stick. Movie stars make up most of our top five choices with local girls scoring at the bottom of the list. We've grown up with them so there is less mystery and appeal. We're two teenaged virgins, tasting independence for the first time.

When I'm around town I'm treated like a hero. Adults stop and speak and children act like I'm their buddy. Of course I virtually ignore them, which makes them follow me even more, tagging along behind me as I go into the post office to get the mail or across the street to Ron Canning's little grocery store for a dozen eggs.

"When is your next fight, Duff?" they ask. "Don't know," I reply.

"You going to knock out whoever it is?" they ask. "Maybe," I reply.

Danny snickers at this little troop of runny-nosed seven-year-olds and Dewey calls me the Pied Piper of Parrsboro.

At the beginning of August I fall in love. It happens when a bunch of us are hanging around a busy Main Street, bustling with Saturday night shoppers. Down the street come the girls from school with a new face among them. The first time I see Vivien Schuster, something happens inside me. The hormone tap, slowly dripping since the beginning of my adolescence, turns into a torrent. I can feel my heart racing.

She is tall. Taller than me with dark brown hair. She is very beautiful. When she first flashes her green eyes in my direction I go weak in the knees. As if Jack Ryan has just landed a solid one.

"She's from Connecticut, visiting her Aunt Kate and she's here for two weeks and I suppose you think she's cute," says Lois Tupper indignantly.

"She's more than cute, she's gorgeous," I answer.

"Oh, she thinks she's it," replies Lois and stomps off up the street.

Despite the old man's warning, hero worship is making me cocky. I walk right up to her. She is with the girls from Eastern Avenue, Donna Ackles and her friends. As I approach, she gives me this knowing look, half smiling with her eyebrows slightly arched — I think they call it bemused. I tell her I'll be happy to show her around Parrsboro. The other girls nudge and wink at each other. She smiles at me mostly with those incredible eyes that — I swear — could draw the caulking out of deck planking.

"Well, I'm not certain there is much to see."

"Oh you're wrong," I say. "There is lots to see, all kinds of hidden treasures."

Her next question fills me with terror, but I'm in too far to back out now. In front of girls I've known all my life, I'm making a fool of myself and hardly care. "How old are you?" she asks, coolly appraising me. My face reddens as if I'm grazed again by the fast leather of an eight-ounce glove.

There is no point lying. Her cousin, Donna, and her friends can hardly conceal their eagerness to blab. So, faced with telling the truth, I stretch it for all its worth. I tell her I'm going on seventeen. Actually I turned sixteen five weeks ago, just before the Moncton fight. So

I am on my way to seventeen. In eleven months. She smiles again and with a slightly sophisticated New England accent says those hurtful words a woman will say to a guy, "No thanks."

I can feel my face flushing even more. This calls for an exit with dignity. I do my best to keep my composure. My footwork, thank God, doesn't fail me. I do an abrupt turn as I say, "If you change your mind, I'll be around."

She does change her mind. The next week we meet by accident near the drug store and she says, "I'll take you up on your offer if you're still interested." Still interested! Oh, if she only knew. Every morning she is the first image of my day. Every night I hug my pillow and pretend the two of us are in a passionate embrace, with those eyes now acknowledging and totally confirming I am the dream of her life.

That afternoon she sits on the crossbar of my bike and I take her to a place called Jeffers Falls, just outside of town on the Beaverdam Road. It's my favorite hideaway where I can trout fish and think and get away from boxing. We walk in the shallow waters of the pool below the falls. She picks wild flowers and we watch some big trout swaying back and forth in the cool green water.

She tells me about her life and family.

"My father is in the insurance business. It's his sister who lives here. Do you know Aunt Kate?"

"Only to see her. Your father grew up in the States?"

"Yes, we're not rich but we have a nice house just outside Hartford. I went to a private school until I was fourteen, but felt I was isolating myself from the real world. My mother objected but I was right. Private schools shelter you."

She looks up the steep rock wall surrounding the falls.

"I could go up that." She pauses. "With the right equipment."

"You climb cliffs?" I ask.

"I've done a bit of it. I told you I don't want to be sheltered."

"Ever sailed?"

"No, but I'd like to learn. My grandfather was a New England sea captain, who took his wife and children to sea."

"I'm sorry I missed that era," I reply.

"You would have been a pirate. Mind you, a very well-mannered one."

She laughs often and her voice is soft, musical. I listen with total attention, catching every nuance of every word. She wades back in the pool again, lifting her cotton dress above her knees. Even on the rocky bottom, her movements are liquid, effortless, like a stream finding its way around mossy rocks.

She takes my hand as we sit on the big rocks at the edge of the water.

"You have soft hands for a boxer," she says. "You know something else? You have a very good vocabulary, for your age." She laughs again and drops my hand and jumps off the rock, wading up to her knees. Behind her the rushing water of the falls sends a fine spray into the air. The sun is shining and somehow she fits this place perfectly as if she is born to be here. I sit watching her with water behind her dropping the ninety feet into the pool and I smile back. "A good vocabulary." I can hardly put a half dozen words together. I am smitten, I know it and she knows it too. Laughing, she suddenly comes towards me. Walking out of the water without saying a word, she kisses me. It is the best afternoon of my life.

8

THE CUBANS ARE COMING

Vivien has one more week in Parrsboro and we're together every day. We walk on the beach and go for long bike rides. I take her to visit my favorite places, a quiet country stream where we sit under a big pine tree waiting for the rain to stop. We picnic in a patch of woods where a rabbit jumps out, startling her. On top of Kirk Hill we look down on miles of blueberry fields at the feet of the Cobequid Mountains. I take her out in the catboat on a beautiful afternoon. She scoops her hand into the basin and soaks me with the salt water, laughingly calling me Captain Bligh. When I kiss her, she is warm and submissive. In the hot August woods we hold hands until our fingers are drenched and need to be wiped on the soft moss. We kiss and fondle often. She never lets me go all the way, but she lets me go farther than I've ever been before. When I touch her in intimate places she draws away. This is agonizing but when I finally complain she tells me, "Duff, I'm scared. What if I get pregnant? This is not what I want to drop on my parents. I want to be a teacher and when the time is right I want to have your baby."

On her last night in town we walk in the fields behind Parrsboro. She weeps when I tell her I love her. It's something I've never said before. She tells me she'll always love me. We are smitten, heartsick and already missing each other. When she leaves I'm empty, wretched.

Dewey isn't finding love this summer but he does find a job, working at the mill making four dollars and fifty cents a day. I take the catboat out by myself to sail across the bay, anchor and write long letters to Vivien. And as I grow more confident with the boat, I go farther from home. Some days I slip the ropes and leave on the morning tide before dawn while the town is still in darkness.

A few times I scare myself. I start dreaming about Vivien and get caught in a rip where fierce swirling waters of the incoming tide drive the catboat sideways, spinning it around. I lose control near Cape Split, where the tidal rip nearly puts me on the rocks. I think I'm going to die as the jagged black fingers of the cliff loom closer. I can smell the salty seaweed and wet pungent minerals of sea stones. I can also smell my own fear as the boat lurches almost beyond control.

Finally, away from the rocks and rips, I realize as a sailor I must do better; I want to be able to handle this boat in any situation. It's midnight when I sail into Parrsboro. The water is very calm and the moonlight lets me make out the two people waiting on the wharf. Dewey and his father are there.

Helping me tie up, Lloyd only says I've been gone a long time and gets in his truck. He is unhappy.

"Dad doesn't like you taking the boat so much," Dewey says. "He's scared you'll drown and your old man will blame him."

"I'm careful. I love that boat. If I had the money I'd buy one just like it."

"Duff, it's almost September. The weather is going to get worse and the old man was really worried tonight. God, you've been gone all day. Your mother called twice."

The two of us still go out weekends but Lloyd wants us back by four in the afternoon. Autumn winds blow up the basin, the spray is cold and the boat churns and bobs. Sailing is now harder work, the movements more reckless but the experience more rewarding.

School starts and suddenly boxing comes back with a vengeance. I arrive home one afternoon and the old man and my mother are sitting at the kitchen table drinking tea. My mother's class is out early so I'm not surprised to see her home but the old man doesn't come home in the afternoons unless we're sparring after school and we haven't been doing much of that lately.

"Well, Champ, how would you like to fight in Halifax?"

He has given me a lot of slack since Moncton. Pats me on the back and calls me champ. Every mention of the fight, including all the critical reports, he's saved. All the clippings in the New Brunswick and Nova Scotia newspapers are in his cluttered den, stacked on his small desk beneath a photograph of him smiling, with his arm around Joe Louis. For my mother the most troubling part of the Moncton fight is a picture of me leaving the ring with people bending over my unconscious opponent. It ran in the *Halifax Herald* and was even in *Maclean's Magazine* with a critical article about boys boxing. Standing there looking at my old man, I realize how much boxing has been out of my life this summer. There is that intensity in his eyes that tells me it has not been far from him. He looks at me over his glasses, waiting for a response. My mother doesn't say a word. Her hair is pulled back, highlighting the silver temples that give her such a distinguished look. My mother has been called regal but today she just looks distressed.

"Halifax?"

"Yeah, the Cubans are coming to Canada for a series of exhibition fights and Halifax is one of their stops. Leo Cormier saw you fight in Moncton. He thought you were pretty damn good. You interested in finding out how good you really are?"

"You think I'm ready for that? You always told me Cubans are the best in the world."

He gives me that look of his.

"If I didn't think you could do it, I would have told him no. The thing is, after playing with that little boat all summer or clinging to that Yankee girl, are you up to it? It will be a lot of work to get ready and, buddy, you ain't ready."

So I'm back in full training, lugging my five-pounders around the four-mile square. Sometimes on sunny weekends when I run, I see the catboat clearing the lighthouse with its white sail just under the clouds, full and free. It becomes a speck and disappears in the distance.

The fight is set for October fifth at the Halifax Forum. Head protectors will be used. They block my vision and bother my sense of freedom, but I have no choice. The old man says headgear is now a fact of life. Parents and politicians are demanding it. As he puts it, "Those in charge of boxing are buckling under."

The Cubans and Canadians will be the under-card before a couple of middleweight professional fights — one involves a Canadian champ who is putting his title on the line. This guarantees a full house.

My letters to Vivien have gone from one a day to two a week. She writes all the time. We even talk on the phone long distance but the old man is on me about the cost. I'm lovesick, heartsick and worried, and it's the worry that now drives me.

I'm home from school, into my trunks and an hour in the basement on the bag. Then into my running clothes and two hours of roadwork. By then the old man is home. We eat, I do homework and we box with a new intensity. Maybe he's worried about the Cubans too. He hits me hard so I start hitting him harder. Gone are the love taps of early training. We are throwing solid, stinging punches.

One evening my mother comes to the basement to tell him he's wanted on the telephone. She watches and cries, "You're hurting each other. That's enough!"

Her cry breaks the spell. My father looks at me. My face is stinging and I can feel my heart pounding. There is a tiny smatter of blood under his nose. I didn't notice it until he stopped moving and it trickles down to his mouth as he stands there, breathing hard, staring at me with a look I've never seen before. A look of sadness, as if to say he's sorry. He steps out of the ring, taking off his gloves as he goes up to answer the phone. My mother also has a curious expression. Without a word she comes over to me and hugs me hard. It's the last time my father and I spar.

Now guys from the club come over, which is good because otherwise our house has become unusually quiet. Danny spends a lot of time with me, training in the ring and on the road. The old man even gets Mouse Morrison to spar with me. He is told to show no mercy. Big Mouse fills the little boxing ring in our basement. He's clumsy and slow and I stay out of his way as much as possible but when he tags me it hurts. Could a sixteen-year-old Cuban hit harder than a heavyweight like Mouse? When we're sparring Mouse murmurs, as if he's carrying on a conversation with himself but I think he's taking out his frustration on me. He's having a rotten summer. He was disqualified in his last fight in Amherst when he put a head-lock on his opponent and refused to let go, even with the old man

37

and Curly screaming at him. The fans were laughing their heads off and the ref was going nuts but Mouse continued to cling to his opponent's neck, nearly suffocating him. It's just another thing for the old man to live down. After that Mouse showed up at our house almost every day to apologize until my mother intervened and invited him in to supper. Under extreme pressure from her, the old man finally told Mouse to forget it and have some grub. Later, as Mouse was leaving and my mother was out of earshot, the old man told him if he ever did it again, he'd kill him.

At six foot two and two hundred pounds Mouse is a powerful guy. In school he doesn't always get things right. He's ready to drop out but can't make up his mind whether to join the army or the navy. Every day it's a different decision. The old man is pushing the navy but the truth is, Mouse isn't great on the water. He doesn't like boats. We took him out on the catboat and had hardly cleared the harbor when he got sick and we had to bring him ashore. He couldn't wait to get off and leaped for the ladder of the wharf before we tied up. The rungs were wet and slippery and Mouse dropped below the surface like a load of stones. Laughing, Danny told him he needed to wash the puke off his clothes anyway, to which a soggy and irate Mouse yelled, "You got some fucking nerve talking about puke, Mr. King of the Pukers." Mouse should pick the army.

He's having woman problems too.

"Why," he whines, "do girls always leave me when I'm so nice to them?" We're doing roadwork, running together beside a pasture a mile from town. Grazing cattle lift their heads to listen to Mouse's lament.

"Nice to them?" I reply. "You left Roberta Byers at the dance Saturday night. Just left her there and went off with the guys. No wonder she won't speak to you."

"But she knows I can't dance," Mouse pleads.

"Look, Mouse, you take a girl to a dance, she expects you to take her home. She expects you to buy her a pop and she expects you to dance with her."

Sweat rolling down his big forehead, Mouse lifts his head to the sky and screams, "That's too much to expect!" Down the road a cow moos as if in agreement. We both laugh.

By October first I feel fit. I've never worked so hard. Am I using the training to mask the way I miss Vivien or am I just desperately scared of facing a Cuban? Since I was three the old man has built up Cuba as the home of great boxers. There may be something else. I came home from Moncton a hero and let's face it, I liked it. I can fool myself but I like the way younger kids look up to me. I like the new-found respect. I like the way the old man calls me "champ." I don't want to lose that feeling.

Wearing heavy army boots to built up my legs, I usually do one and a half times around the four-mile square then walk the last two miles. Some of my friends in one of their father's cars will follow me, shouting encouragement. Sometimes youngsters, ten- and twelve-year-olds, will run for a mile or so then drop out. A couple of young teachers and Danny sometimes run with me on Saturdays. People watch as I pass through town. They know I'm facing a Cuban opponent and they often shout encouragement as we pass: "Good luck, Duff!"

By now the air has changed and autumn breezes keep me cooler. One boot ahead of the other, mile after mile, one five pounder then the next. My legs ache.

The day of the fight we take the old man's car to Halifax. Curly and the old man in front, with Danny, Mouse and me in the back. Dewey still does not have his father's permission to attend, so the others are my cheering section. My mother says she can't bear it and hugs me hard at the front door. "Please be careful."

It's a twisting, turning road to Halifax. Every so often it can pull into a straight stretch then return to tight curves. For the first fifty miles it runs somewhat parallel to the water and the basin keeps appearing and disappearing. I watch the blueberry fields and small farms of Cumberland County slide by and wonder if I'll be coming back a winner with my hero status confirmed. Suddenly a big bug hits the windshield with a splatter.

"Late in the year for those things," the old man comments.

"That's what you're going to do to that Cuban, eh, Duff," Curly says, turning to me.

The others laugh. We're at the edge of the basin, just before the road winds inland, and I look back as far as I can, searching for a catboat with its sail catching the wind.

39

9

MOUSE AND THE HOOKER

They have a reception for all the Cubans and Canadians. It's a big room packed with people. The adults are having wine and beer as the fighters wander around with soft drinks, meeting each other. It's awkward because we can't really talk. There are several interpreters and we stand around as they translate.

When I meet my opponent he seems very shy. As we shake hands Mouse strides up to me, holding a beer. He is two years under-age for drinking but his size distorts the fact he's only nineteen. Mouse is very pleased with himself. He looks at my opponents and says, "He's too cute to hit." Even the interpreter laughs, only the Cuban doesn't catch on. Fact is, he does seem rather pretty for a boy. His name is Hernandez Mitz and he's sixteen. We exchange comments through the interpreter. I ask him how long he's been boxing and while I'm trying my best to carry on a conversation with someone who doesn't speak English, Mouse and Danny are having a great time, saying things like, "I'm no homo but Duff's opponent is pretty enough to date."

On and on they go. Yak, yak, yak. When you're not fighting there is plenty of reason to be relaxed.

"If the old man sees you with a beer, he'll give you shit."

"No he won't," Mouse declares, while staying as far away as possible from the old man in the crowded room. Mouse has downed two beers by the time the old man finally notices him.

"Put that beer down or start walking home, young man."

Considering it's a three hour drive to Parrsboro, Mouse puts the beer down but it's empty anyway. By the time the reception is over he's also managed to put away two glasses of wine.

The dressing rooms are down the corridor from the reception and there are plenty of people milling around outside as I change. Danny and Mouse are in and out as Curly tapes my hands. Curly, who my mother says at the best of times has a vacant look in his eyes, has had a couple of beers and keeps burping as he's doing up my gloves. The door to the corridor is left open and I see Mouse talking to these two women. They're wearing tight dresses, high heels and plenty of makeup, although they don't look much older than Mouse. The old man comes down the corridor and passes Mouse and the women.

"That's all we need. Him involved with hookers," he declares.

"Hookers?" I say. I've never seen prostitutes before. "Are you sure?" I ask.

"Kid, believe me, I know a hooker when I see one. I wish I'd left Mouse home."

On my thirteenth birthday my mother gave me a pocket dictionary. I often carry it with me and when I have nothing to do I look up words. Kind of a hobby of mine. I think the word for the fight against Hernandez Mitz is "anticlimactic." After all the work, the hours getting ready, the running and sparring and thinking about this fight, it's over in no time. We both fire a few punches but I'm hardly warmed up when it's over. It's the dullest fight I ever had and the judges called it a draw. I feel empty.

Younger fighters are first on the card, so after I shower I have plenty of time to watch the rest of the bouts. Danny is sitting alone with a smile on his face.

"Good fight. You should have won," he says.

When I ask where everybody is he snickers.

"Your father and Curly are sitting over on the other side. As for Mouse — " He points way up to the very back seats near the rafters. The Halifax Forum holds five thousand people but is less than half

41

full tonight, and the back rows are empty except for Mouse and the two hookers sitting on either side of him. Mouse waves at me and even at that distance I can see his toothy smile.

"What's he doing?"

"Trying to get a blow job," Danny answers.

"You're kidding?"

"No, he's trying to beat them down to ten dollars. That's all he has and they want twenty."

We spend more time looking back at Mouse than we do watching the fight. Suddenly Danny jabs me in the ribs.

"Look," he says.

There is just one girl sitting next to Mouse and the other one has disappeared.

"God, she's doin' it right here," Danny shouts.

"She can't be, not here."

The next moment the girl raises her head.

Danny is beside himself.

"Can you believe it? Right here."

"They're just fooling around. They must be."

"He's gettin' it," Danny shouts over the crowd noise. "Mouse is gettin' it. Right here. Oh my God, he's gettin' it."

Five minutes later Mouse is standing in the aisle next to us with a sheepish grin on his big face.

Danny is very excited. He jumps up and shakes Mouse's hand, pumping it vigorously, congratulating him. Danny acts like Mouse just scaled Mount Everest or something. "Mouse, I couldn't believe it," he says. "You got blown in the Halifax Forum."

"Not all the way," Mouse says as he sits down.

"What do you mean?" Danny asks.

"Just what she calls ten dollars worth." He looks at us and smiles, "But it was better than nothing."

I'm thinking this is going to make the rounds in Parrsboro faster than a grass fire in a summer breeze. It's going to mean more flak for the old man who is responsible for us, I guess. I grow slightly uncomfortable thinking he may have been right. He should have left Mouse at home.

Most of the fights are boring and end in draws. The boxers are restrained, never really letting go. The crowd is restrained as well.

42

Maybe the booze has made them mellow. Mouse is dozing in the seat next to me. It's only the final fight that generates much enthusiasm. It's a title fight for the Canadian Middleweight championship. The challenger is the crowd favorite. He's a fisherman from Nova Scotia's eastern shore who throws some heavy punches that stagger the champ. Eventually the champ, a Montreal fighter by the name of Kid Carter, recovers and lands a big left hook that brings the crowd to its feet and produces some wild cheering as the fisherman gamely fights back. He loses and the fight card is over.

Two thousand people are filing out of the Forum. Danny is beside me and Mouse is just ahead of us. When we reach the wide corridor, Mouse sees his two lady friends and heads towards them. I go to pick up my things in the dressing room. Two minutes later I'm back in the crowded corridor just in time to see a policemen take one of the women, the one Mouse is most friendly with, by the arm. I can't hear what they're saying because of the noise but she's protesting and the policemen takes both her shoulders, spins her around and starts pushing her down the corridor. She struggles to get free, then Mouse grabs the policemen's arm and, oh God, there's trouble.

People are pushed into each other. Mouse has the policemen in a headlock and the two of them twist and wrestle into the crowd.

"Let him go." I hear the old man's voice over the crowd noise. "Let him go, Mouse!"

The old man and Curly try to get to Mouse and the cop through the crowd but now police are everywhere, grabbing Mouse and dragging him away as the woman shrieks at the top of her voice.

"You goddamn cops." With that she's literally picked off her feet by two beefy policemen. She's screaming and swearing like I've never heard a woman swear, words Lawrence doesn't even use. A cop has a grip on the old man's arm and they're both talking excitedly as the woman shrieks again. Curly's been in the tussle too — his comb-over, that one piece of hair across his otherwise bald head, is standing straight up. People in the crowd are now turning surly and giving the cops a hard time.

"Three cops against one woman. Good work, boys," they yell sarcastically above the confusion, cursing and pushing. I believe it's what you call a donnybrook. The cop and the old man aren't moving, they're just talking excitedly while holding on to each other like they're doing a slow dance. Suddenly the cop nods and lets go of the old man's arm. The old man turns to Curly. There is fire in his eyes.

"Get the boys. We're leaving." We drive to the police station and I've never seen the old man so angry. It's a good thing Mouse isn't here because he's getting an awful tongue lashing right now. The plan was to go for Chinese food after the fight, the old man's treat. Instead we spend the next hour and a half hanging around the police station as he negotiates Mouse's release.

There is no Chinese food. We get Mouse, who looks terrified when he walks out of the holding cell and meets the glare of the old man. As we drive through the outskirts of the city, Mouse tries to apologize but the old man explodes.

"Don't talk to me," he roars. "You're a fucking idiot!"

No one says another word. It starts to rain and we sit there in the dark car as the wipers go back and forth. As I listen to the rhythm of the rubber sliding across the wet windshield, gradually their repetitive sound turns into words. The wipers seem to be saying, "You can take him in two, you can take him in two, you can take him in two." There is an occasional cough, but otherwise not a human sound as we drive through the night.

10

THE OLD MAN'S RECOGNITION

The old man and Mouse don't make up this time. Mouse doesn't come back to the club and the story of the blow job, the police and the hooker is all over town. It's the last straw for some parents. People start taking their sons out of the club, saying it's a bad influence.

The old man isn't taking it well. Boxing is his life and the club is his pride and joy. My mother worries about him. Over lunch one day when he's at the store, she tells me the doctor has warned him about high blood pressure. That was before the summer, before Moncton and Halifax, and she says he's not eating like he should.

"Help him through this, Duff, even if you're tired of training so hard. I know there are other things you would like to do, but right now stand by your father."

Stand by him I do. The Henwood brothers, Frankie and Johnny, are my main sparring partners. They are twins, a year older than me. They look alike, but you can tell them apart in the ring. Johnny is a much harder puncher and Frankie is faster.

Dewey and I refinish the catboat over the winter. We spend hours sanding the wooden hull in his father's boathouse. Sometimes Danny helps and Mouse even shows up occasionally. Mouse never mentions the old man.

My father has his detractors but he also has his supporters. There are plenty of people who think the boxing club has been good for Parrsboro. We've had three boxers who gained a certain reputation, and one even turned professional for a while. Over the years the club has given the town lots of good publicity. It's only the last few months, with the knockouts in Moncton and Mouse's antics in Amherst and Halifax, that things have gone sour. Lawrence comes in one Saturday when Dewey and I are sanding away. He says the old man has the support of most people and a lot of them think it's time he was recognized for his work in the club. This doesn't sound like Lawrence but Dewey says the unthinkable has happened. Lawrence has a girlfriend.

"He certainly seems more kind-hearted."

"Yep," Dewey says. "It works wonders."

As the winter months slip by, the boxing club is in low gear. We're down to seven members and hold only one card against the Amherst club. I fight a guy named Billard. He's pretty good but is open to my left, which I've been working on to make stronger. It's a good night for the club. I win, both Henword brothers win and so does Danny. Parrsboro takes five out of seven, with one win for Amherst and one draw.

A week later, Curly stops me in front of the fish and meat market.

"Ya know what?" he says, fixing one eye on me while the other looks off down Main Street. "Alex is going to be given a special award for running the club."

Over a cup of tea my mother confirms it. The Lions Club is holding a civic recognition night, handing out three awards for community work and the old man is getting one of them.

"Apparently some people think your father has received a raw deal."

"You don't?" I ask.

She shrugs and only says, "Boxing is a brutal sport and many people will see that before your father."

As for him, he's a hoot about things like this. He tries to act as if he doesn't care about the recognition, which causes even my mother to smirk and wink at me. He cares. He's as proud as a peacock. It's the only time he pays any attention to his clothes.

"What am I going wear?" he keeps asking my mother, who keeps telling him she'll look after it.

"You've got three weeks, Alex. Relax."

"Will I have to make a speech?"

"Yes, you'll have to say something, something appropriate."

They argue over what he'll say. He wants to use the night to fire back at his critics and she is absolutely against any, what's the word — retaliation.

I'm never sure if the old man is serious or just teasing her. He can be a big tease and he gets her going when he comes into the kitchen with a pencil and pad and reads what he's written for the big night.

"You're saying no such thing."

"It's payback time," he snarls, but with a half grin and a light in his eyes that tells me he isn't really serious. Maybe this is what he'd like to say but he knows he won't say it.

A week before the civic recognition there is a big school dance. Paying attention to footwork since I was three led me into dancing. I'm not the best dancer in the school but as Lois Tupper says, "For a boy you're not bad."

They announce a lady's choice, a way to get guys dancing instead of standing around looking goofy, according to Lois who organizes these things.

Suddenly Heather Harrington is standing next to me.

"Dance with me, Duff?"

She could dance with any guy in the place and I'm flattered she's picked me. We waltz. She smells wonderful. I'm trying to think if it's proper to tell a girl she smells good. I don't want her to be offended or worse, to think I go around smelling girls.

My mother always says, "Nothing ventured, nothing gained."

"Heather, you smell wonderful."

It's definitely the right thing to say. She grips my hand tighter and we move a little closer.

We dance the rest of the evening. Heather is developed and I can feel her full breasts under her red sweater. Her hair is honey blond and she has big brown eyes. After the dance I walk her home. She lives ten minutes farther down the Whitehall Road and on her front steps we kiss. First, a peck on the cheek, then a short kiss on the lips, then a full embrace and another kiss and another. She draws away from me and smiles.

"I've wanted to kiss you for a long time."

I walk off her steps, dizzy and breathless.

Halfway home, through the moonlit snow with my steps making a crunching sound, I remember Vivien. I'm an unfaithful, traitorous bastard.

THE OLD MAN'S
FINAL ROUND

I've been working at the hardware store all winter. There is always stock to be unpacked and customers to look after. Dewey sometimes helps me. We've just about finished the catboat to the everloving joy of my mother. Sanding a hull is dirty work and every weekend my clothes, skin and hair are covered in layers of dust.

The day of the banquet, I'm up early, as the old man is having his picture taken and then attending a noon luncheon hosted by the town. My mother has bought him a dark blue suit and made him get a haircut. The usual white fringe hanging over his face is shortened and slicked back. The white stubble is gone. He's ready for the photographer.

Lawrence drops by just as he's leaving the store.

"God, Alex, nobody will know you."

"Very funny. Get rid of that beer gut and I'll give ya this suit someday."

The evening banquet is upstairs over Burke's Restaurant on Main Street. The old man is at the head table with the other recipients. Jerry Forbes is a popular barber who runs the little league baseball program. May Farrell has been the town hall clerk as long as anyone can remember.

There are speeches and toasts and applause as each of the honorees is introduced. Dewey and his parents are there; his father is past-president of the Lions Club. As the old man is introduced I watch Lloyd Hunter out of the corner of my eye, just to see his reaction. Relations are strained since Moncton, but he applauds as the old man gets up and takes a bow.

I have seen my father in many different situations: so mad he could punch a referee, so embarrassed you could see his beet-red face a mile away, but this is the first time I've ever heard him give a speech that isn't an angry harangue at young boxers. This is a polite speech as opposed to his screaming in the club. He is speaking in a low, flat voice. He is sincere, thanking the Lions and the town and giving a brief history of the boxing club. He singles out Curly, who is sitting close to us. It's the first time I've ever seen Curly wearing a shirt and tie. He's with his sister, his only family, and when the old man thanks him for his work in the club, Curly smiles as if someone has just given him a million dollars.

The old man never changes his tone; he keeps speaking in a low, steady voice. He says the boxing program has had some setbacks but with the support of the town he hopes to keep the club going. It's a good speech and he gets a big ovation.

Dewey has a big, box-like flash camera he just bought in a secondhand store in Amherst, one of those places filled with wooden boxes and old furniture and smelling of dust and decay. The old guy who sold him the camera gave him a lot of old flashbulbs and occasionally one will blow up with a soft pop and reddish-blue flame.

"I got them for nothing," he explains. "Most of them work even though they're ten years old and have been in the guy's basement for half a dozen years. It's a wonder any of them work."

Dewey really likes photography and jumps up and down snapping pictures of the old man as he promised my mother he'd do. As the banquet wraps up, the guests of honor pose for more photographs, holding their plaques. People are milling around watching the process. The old man is in the middle of the group, holding his plaque as the photographer for the *Amherst Daily News* gets them organized. I'm smiling at him when suddenly he grabs himself, pulling at his white shirt, then he looks towards my mother who is standing a few feet away. He tries to say something to her as he pulls hard at his shirt; he takes a step forward and topples over, not using his hands to break the fall. There are shouts and cries and my mother screams and runs toward him. I am paralyzed. My feet won't move. People are bending over my stricken father. One of the town doctors is a member of the Lions Club. I hear him say, "Call an ambulance."

I hear my mother crying, "Alex, Alex, Alex."

Curly has tears in his eyes and people are running to get blankets and a pillow. I can't get through the crowd and I don't really try. I stand on the outside of the circle of people around my father. Bits and pieces of a dozen conversations fill the air. "Heart attack" and "hospital" and "a bad one" — words are entering my brain as I stand there waiting for him to get up. Finally they are lifting him on a stretcher. The doctor tells my mother to come along. I am left there.

Dewey, Curly and I walk to the hospital; we don't talk. When we get there my mother is nowhere to be seen. The nurse tells us she's with my father. We wait. It is 9:20 and the three of us sit and make small talk but really don't say much. At 10:40 my mother walks out of the room. She is ashen and crying. One look at her tells me he's dead.

"Duff," she sobs. "He's gone. I'm sorry, I should have known you'd be here. Why didn't they tell me?" She wipes her tears. "Maybe they did and I didn't hear. I don't know. He's gone, Duff. Do you want to be with him for a while?"

I sit alone in the hospital room staring at my father. Death is so definite. I know he isn't coming back and while there are tears in my eyes over my loss there is great guilt because deep within me there is a sudden sense of relief. I can't stop it, the guilt can't drive it out. I keep seeing the last time we boxed and that smatter of blood under his nose and the way he looked at me, the sadness and surprise in his eyes. I try to figure out what he was thinking just before my mother ordered us to stop. I wonder if he was back in his navy boxing days and her shouts had brought him back to earth. He looked at me and realized it was his son he was fighting, not some opponent: his honest to God, flesh and blood son. And where was I? Was it my father I was boxing or was I striking out at the tension and frustration I sometimes feel? Boxing is all about training and training means giving

51

up a lot of things. Was I striking at him or what he had imposed on me?

His funeral is big, the church full. His favorite hymn, "Rock Of Ages," floats out the doors and over the little town. There are kind words about community service and family and a good man. I stand at the graveside and watch his black casket slip out of sight. Eight . . . nine . . . ten. He isn't getting up.

When we get back to our house there are two dozen cars around it. The kitchen and living room are filled with people: Dewey and his parents, Heather and her mother, Curly, Lawrence, Danny, the Henwood brothers, teachers from school, people from the church, my mother's closest friends. I barely acknowledge them. I go to the basement and put on my running clothes and my army boots and leave by the back door.

I walk up the road then I start to run, through the back streets, along upper Main Street and around the four-mile square. It's bitterly cold and soon my lungs are on fire but I keep running. The old man is down for the count.

1 2

THE WEDDING

Six months after the funeral, my mother sells the hardware store to the Baxter brothers from Springhill. The old man's estate left me forty-five hundred dollars. My mother wants me to use the money for college. I have other plans. Much to her objections I want to buy a boat. She is even more indignant when I tell her I'm going to box professionally. It's what I know, what I've trained for. I've spent too much time getting ready not to try.

"You sound like your father," she replies.

"Yes, I know." I'm in his study looking at the photographs. I'm drawn here often.

"Have you ever noticed in all these photographs of Joe Louis, he never smiles? He always has the same look on his face."

"Yes, Duff, I have." She comes and stands beside me. "Have a good look at his expression," she says. "He doesn't look like a happy man, does he? And, he was what, heavyweight champion of the entire world. Please, Duff, please don't. You can do so much more than box."

Curly keeps the club going as best he can. There's just the Henwood brothers, Bob Woolaver, Danny, and me but we win our fights. I lead the roadwork and we follow the old man's routine, around the

53

four-mile square three times a week, then push-ups, sparring, working the heavy bag and skipping. We train as if he is with us. Sometimes when we're running, I look up to the front of the group, thinking I'll see him leading the pack. The back of his neck would be red. He'd be winded but he'd never stop.

Inadvertently, my mother increases my desire to sail. For my seventeenth birthday she gives me a book about a man named Slocum from Nova Scotia who sailed alone around the world. I think a lot about what that must have been like, alone in all that ocean. Spending a Sunday in the catboat I imagine going down the U.S. coast to the West Indies and Central America. Newspaper ads with boats for sale pile up in a corner of my bedroom.

In the year after my father's death my roadwork takes a course closer to the sea. I am now drawn to the water in a new way. Running along the beach I think of it as my friend. It represents both new horizons and my past, my parents, the swirling rip tide of the old man and the serene surface of my mother. Sometimes I stop to watch the sunset on the ocean and a yearning comes over me to go, to climb aboard a three-masted schooner and sail away. It doesn't take much imagination to see one coming over the horizon, coming to get me.

My mother and I are tired and talked out. We reach an understanding. She cannot accept boxing and I will not accept college or even much more high school. My marks are falling and my interest is gone off somewhere, out there on the waves. She cannot change me anymore than she could change my father. After months of almost bitter arguments she finally accepts this and we begin a new and better time for both of us.

I still think I hear him. Some evenings when I approach the house I expect to see him walk past a window. Sometimes the memories aren't pleasant. They often center on our hard hitting and that blood under his nose. His expression still haunts me. What was he thinking as he looked at me: pride, disappointment, love? I train hard and I fight hard. In fifteen months I've won in Moncton, twice in Amherst and three times in Port Greville. I'm strong and ready and want to turn pro. I'm not sure if it's my dream or his but it's all I've got.

The big news comes in late September. Dewey and Danny show up at the house one evening.

"You'll never guess." Danny looks at me with that mass of sandy hair flopping over his forehead. Dewey straddles a kitchen chair and smiles, "Get ready, you're going to a wedding."

"I am?"

"You certainly are."

"And just who's getting married?"

They look at each other and shout, "Lawrence!"

My mother calls it unbelievable. Lawrence has always been a loner. His parents died when he was young and his elderly aunt raised him. He left school in grade six and has fished since then. He is what my mother would call an underachiever. Things changed last summer when Lawrence was seen in the company of Agnes Atkinson, first at the movies watching Randolph Scott, then out driving Sunday afternoons. Then the sure sign of love. Lawrence started washing his truck before he'd pick up Agnes. When Lawrence buys a new red and black checkered shirt at Resnicks and gets a shave at Jerry's Barber Shop, people say he's going to pop the question. He does. The wedding is set for October twenty-second.

Dewey, Danny and me decide to chip in on a wedding present. Danny says Lawrence needs a new chain saw, but we can't afford it. Besides, my mother says we need something more appropriate. We settle on a toaster.

"Lawrence needs a toaster," says Dewey. "It will stop him tearing off a chunk of bread and sticking his hand in the fire."

A week before the wedding Lawrence shows up at our house.

"How ya doin'?" he says.

"Lawrence, come in."

"Na." He half turns, looking away from me. "You goin' to the wedding, right?"

"Sure I am. I'm one of the ushers, remember?"

"Yeah, I remember. I was wondering if you could give the toast, you're good with words."

"The toast."

"Yeah."

"What toast?" I ask.

"The one after the first one," he replies.

"What do I say?"

"Whatever you want."

For the first time he looks me straight in the eye. "Okay?"

"Sure," I reply.

My mother figures Lawrence wants me to give the response to the toast to the bride. "It doesn't have to be long," she says.

"Don't worry. It won't be."

The wedding is at Trinity United Church in Parrsboro, a large wooden building at the foot of Queen Street, where Lawrence has never darkened the door. Agnes and her mother, on the other hand, are regulars and the town is buzzing over what people call a very strange union. Little Agnes is a matchstick of a woman with neat brown hair. She sings in the choir and is quiet and soft-spoken. At the hospital where she works as a practical nurse, patients and staff like her. She is thirty-two years old, doesn't drink, smoke or swear.

Lawrence drinks, smokes, swears, chews tobacco and weighs two hundred pounds with a huge gut hanging over his belt, as if attempting to escape the leather restraint. His red hair is never neat. He is messy, massive and gruff. The church will be packed with the faithful and the curious.

My mother sees all this as a positive influence on Lawrence. Dewey notices also. There is a definite lack of tobacco juice on Lawrence's clothes and the usual small brown blotches at the corners of his mouth have disappeared. The old man would say "humbug" and add you can't change the spots on something or other.

The wedding day is sunny and cold. I have rehearsed my toast until I know it by heart. Dewey's father is going to be Lawrence's best man and Dewey, with his flash camera, will be the official photographer. The minister tells him he doesn't want any pictures taken at the front of the church during the vows. Otherwise he can feel free to walk around and snap away.

As ushers, Danny and I are in our charcoal suits, white shirts and Nova Scotia tartan ties. Dewey, in his Harris Tweed sport coat, is taking pictures of people as they arrive, which clearly delights some and unnerves others.

"Get that camera out of my face, young man," says old Mrs. Howard Smith, lifting her handbag in a threatening manner.

While he's popping away I'm saying what ushers always say — "Friend of the bride? Friend of the groom?" Why don't people just take a seat?

The music is playing, the church is packed and the congregation is standing. Lawrence and Agnes have their heads bowed in prayer when Dewey slides into the pew next to us. He's directly behind Hattie Boyd, who is wearing a huge hat with fawn colored feathers going off at all different angles and protruding a foot behind her head. Lawrence bowed in prayer, Dewey figures, is worth a picture. He's trying to get one over Hattie's shoulder but her hat is in the way. He stands on his tip toes and takes the shot. He doesn't notice that the longest, most slender feather, curved in a wide arch, is almost touching the flashbulb. The prayer ends before he gets the picture and the congregation remains standing to sing Agnes' favorite hymn, "How Great Thou Art." Hattie Boyd is a woman of girth who sings from the heart and she puts a lot into every hymn. Just as Dewey finally snaps the shutter, Hattie lets go a note and throws her head way back, driving the slender feather into the flashbulb that belches and burns with a "poof." Suddenly the feather is on fire, not smoldering but ablaze, the flame racing toward the back of Hattie's head. The church is in full voice. "Then sings my soul . . . "

Stunned, I don't sing but pray, "God, please put out the fire headed for Hattie's head."

The entire hat is on fire, smoke and flames rising from the top of Hattie Boyd. Now other people notice.

"Oh my God!" screams Nancy Cameron in the middle of the hymn. "Hattie, your hat's on fire!"

Instinctively, Hattie reaches up, burns her hand and shrieks. She tries to knock the flaming hat off her head but her hat pins prevent this and she is in total distress. The hymn flounders in confusion and screams. Hattie is running down the aisle with Nancy Cameron and several men, some members of the volunteer fire department, following.

The minister, with his mouth open, tries to make sense of the commotion. Lawrence and Agnes turn to face the congregation, in direct contrast with each other: Lawrence has the beginning of a smile, Agnes the beginning of tears. Hattie can be heard in the vestry and her language is extremely Christian. They finally have the hat off her head but she is still shrieking.

"God! God! Oh Jesus, God!"

The minister finally takes charge. He has Lawrence and Agnes sit in the front pew and he announces the ceremony is suspended for five minutes. At this announcement the rest of the congregation leave their seats in a mad clamor, heading toward the vestry to see if Hattie is all right. Only a stone-faced Dewey sits in the pew.

Hattie's hair is singed and her nerves are shot. She is taken home. People are now asking questions.

"How did it happen?" asks Carmen Gilbert, who goes to all the fires.

"Spontaneous combustion," somebody replies.

"The Lord's doin', do ya think?" someone else asks.

I feel it's best to get this out quickly so when my mother asks me, I tell her it was an accident; Dewey was trying to take a picture. The minister gets people back inside and as he passes the pew he puts a gentle hand on Dewey's shoulder.

"It was an accident, young man. No one doubts that, but maybe after the wedding, we should go see Mrs. Boyd."

At the reception, Hattie is the only topic of conversation amid egg and tuna sandwiches, tea and cake. My toast no longer seems important and Dewey is filled with terror. He pleads with me.

"Don't let me go alone."

"Reverend Hatfield is going with you," I reply.

"Yeah, but I want more than him. Hattie is a big woman!"

So, like lambs to the slaughter, after the reception off we go to Hattie's house. Reverend Hatfield walks slightly ahead of us as if he's leading the condemned to the gallows.

"I could bolt for it right now, Duff, make it to Moncton maybe before midnight and slip into the U.S. tomorrow and never come back."

"Easy, Dewey. It's not that bad."

"Oh no, it's great. I'm the laughingstock of the town again. Knocked out in Moncton then setting a woman on fire at a church wedding. Yeah, this isn't bad at all!"

Hattie has her full frame resting in a large chair with neighbors bringing her tea and sandwiches from the reception. She has been crying and she is angry, very, very angry. Dewey does his best to explain. With his jet black hair in a brush cut, he has a certain military bearing and I think he is rather convincing. While debating his career choices he's considered going into law. As of today, I think he'll rule out photography.

Hattie can not be — what do you call it – placated. She declares flash cameras are dangerous. Dewey could have killed her, could have burned down the church, certainly ruined the wedding. We sit, our heads slightly bowed, listening to Hattie's tirade like convicted arsonists. Reverend Hatfield takes a beating too for allowing cameras in a church. His faith is sorely tested in front of Hattie as he repeatedly tries to smooth things. Finally, in desperation, he suggests a prayer and we listen as he thanks God no one was injured today and asks the Lord to increase our understanding and forgiveness. This is clearly aimed at Hattie and it seems to work. She announces she is a woman of faith and forgiveness and holds no grudges. We get up very much relieved: relieved there are no grudges and more relieved to be going.

The only person who finds humor in all this is Lawrence. He sees us walking home as he and Agnes are leaving for a one night honeymoon in Amherst. He drives alongside and rolls down the window.

"Wonder if we can get Hattie back next year to do that little fire dance on our first anniversary?"

"Lawrence," Agnes scolds, "that's awful."

He howls and drives away, tins cans rattling and "Just Married" written across the back window.

1 3

1 9 5 6

On the first day of November the coal mine explodes in Springhill. The news spreads around town. Danny's mother comes to the front door as we're dropping him off.

"There's been an awful accident at the mine in Springhill."

Dewey turns on the radio in his father's car and gets one of the Halifax stations. The announcer is talking to someone in Springhill. Men are trapped underground; some may be dead; there has been an explosion and a blue flame. Nobody knows much else. As the man in Springhill talks we can hear sirens in the background. A chill runs through me. These miners come to Parrsboro every summer for their annual picnic. It's not that I know them, but they're from the next town — it's as if it's happening here.

The next day we drive the twenty-eight miles to Springhill. The gritty town is full of movement: heavy trucks carry pumps and equipment, emergency vehicles are everywhere. We park on a side street and walk to the pit-head where the great gaping hole leads deep down to the shattered mine. There are hundreds of people standing around in the light rain. Some women are crying, even men have tears in their eyes. Hardly anybody talks except one woman who keeps saying, "They killed our boys, they did. They killed our boys."

Her voice adds to the wet chill.

It is a ghostly scene, people standing by a hole in the ground, waiting for something. There is nothing to do but stand there. Danny, Dewey and I see other people from Parrsboro, their faces wet and tight. There is mostly silence, as if we're trying to hear what's going on under ground. Deep down in the earth rescuers are digging through debris trying to get to the trapped men who may or may not be alive.

A woman near us dabs her eyes. I hear her tell someone her brother is down there. It was his last shift, he was quitting to work on the docks in Halifax. Funny, I think, how life can cheat you — one minute you're ahead then fate slaps you back with a good right hand. The old man used to tell me you have to take life's jabs on the chin. The woman says her brother is just twenty-one. I say a silent prayer for him and the others. It starts to rain hard. By late afternoon we're cold and wet. We walk up to Jimmy Dametre's Candy Store but he's closed. Most of the stores are closed out of respect, Dewey says. The streets are wet as we drive out of town.

When I get home my mother says Heather wants me to call. We have been dating since the dance. We got along so well and had great times together until recently. Now we're arguing and our lives seem to be on separate paths. She's afraid of boats. Her background makes her scared of the water. Then there's boxing. She resents the time I spend training.

I can't compromise, not on training. People don't understand about my boxing. I have to take a shot; it's as much a part of me as my flesh and blood. It was ground right into my soul every time the old man said, "You're going to be good enough to fight professionally. Come on, kid, keep pushing. Let's go for the big time."

Year in and year out. I'd heard it so often I believed it. I still believe it. I fought in Moncton again this year and won a convincing five rounds over a strong opponent. They put the best they have against me and I beat them. I fought in Halifax a month ago and won with a strong left that ended the bout in the third round when my opponent couldn't answer the bell.

I don't phone Heather. Instead I put on my running clothes and head to the beach. I think of those men in Springhill and how their dreams may die tonight with them.

I'm moving along the shore, black water lapping up the beach on my right, gray driftwood polished by waves and wind on my left. Dreams are very much on my mind. Suddenly it comes to me. I've been thinking how to turn pro and also how to satisfy this incredible desire to sail, to see the world, to be a Joshua Slocum, solo sailor and adventurer. I could never co-ordinate these goals. Big time boxing, according to the old man, always meant the United States and it's suddenly so clear. I'll sail to the States, take my gloves and fight along the way. Has anyone ever done it?

In the days that follow nobody gives my idea much of a chance. My mother is adamant, Heather is sulky. Dewey listens but he isn't optimistic.

"Let me put it this way, Duff. If you're going to turn professional you need a full time manager, someone to bring you along."

"I'll get one," I reply, adding that if I win a few fights, managers will come to me. They'll want to sign me up.

Danny thinks its a good idea, but Danny has an ulterior motive. I've noticed the way Danny looks at Heather and sometimes the way she looks at him.

"Watch your flank," Dewey says. "I think Danny is planning a romantic assault."

"The way things are with Heather and me, I wouldn't blame her."

The word here is bravado — I say it but don't really mean it. I'm now uncertain of my feelings for Heather and fear the final break will come when I buy a boat.

Colin Atkinson lives in Advocate Harbour. He was a friend of the old man's and a big fight fan.

"Hear you're looking for a boat."

"Been looking for months. Everything is too old or too expensive."

"I've got a twenty-six footer, a sloop, in good shape."

He wants five thousand dollars for it and we start to dicker right there on Main Street in front of Pearly Wright's Pharmacy. We dicker the next day in Advocate Harbour and the day after that when we take the sloop into the cold November water.

The rugged little boat handles like a dream. We settle on forty-three hundred dollars and conclude the deal with a handshake. I now own a wooden, fore and aft rigged, single mast, twenty-six foot sloop with wheelhouse and galley with a gas stove. It sleeps four and is called the *Martha Jane*. Colin suggests I wait for spring before sailing it up to Parrsboro. He doesn't know me very well. The next morning, sunny and cold, fore and aft sails are full as the sloop pulls along the Parrsboro shore past Spencers Island, Eatonville, Fox River, Port Greville and Diligent River. I am alone, happy and free.

It is almost dark when I get home. Heather is waiting on my porch, standing there in the dusk.

"I want to give you this."

It's a letter. She kisses me on the cheek and leaves without another word. I read it in my room. She is through with me; says she can't compete with boxing and is terrified I'll drown. It is all too much. Too much for her.

My mother has gone to a church meeting and I eat my supper alone in our kitchen reading her letter over and over. The Halifax newspaper is on the table. Thirty-nine miners have died in Springhill.

1 4

1 9 5 7

I'm training with a new intensity; turned nineteen last week, finished school in June and will sail away the first of August. My mother has been crying. Three times now she has broken down and begged me not to go. I plead with her to understand; she refuses, but finally out of exhaustion we stop arguing. This is very hard, I know I'm hurting her and it's the last thing I want to do. I hate myself but I must do this.

Dewey is going on to college. Mouse has joined the army and Dewey is going into law. Danny and Heather are dating now. The three of us are still friends but an element of strain is there. I'm not able to put Heather completely out of my mind.

"She still carries a torch for you," Dewey declares as we sail past Cape Split. "And you know," he says, "the torch is still burning in you."

I bluster and deny it all but can't convince him. He changes the subject.

"How long will you be gone?"

"I haven't even thought of that, of coming back, I mean."

There is a pause.

"By the time I do Heather will be married," I say.

"Not to Danny she won't."

"Why not?"

"There isn't any fire there. Heather is going through the motions with him but I don't think her heart is in it."

We've been taking the *Martha Jane* farther and farther from home, going overnight, making sure the sails and lines are right, that the sloop is absolutely seaworthy. I don't want to hobble back to port forty-eight hours after leaving, dragged in by some fishing boat because I lost a sail, sprung a leak or hit a bad storm. When I go I want to be gone.

Canned goods and water are on board. The sloop has a small Chev engine and I've had to purchase two storage drums for gas. I'd be happy never to turn the engine on but Colin advises me to run it at least once a week. I purchased coastal charts and have read four books on navigation. These overnight excursions give me a chance to study the stars. I have a lot to learn. As departure time gets closer I'm having more doubts. Two things are important to me. I want to leave my mother in a good state of mind and I want to say good bye to Heather alone.

I'm leaving on high tide the first Monday in August, six in the morning. My destination is Boston. All my life the old man talked about Rico's Gym in Boston's Scollay Square. It's where the up-and-comers train and that's where I plan to be. I spend hours pouring over my route down the Minas Basin, into the Minas Channel, through the Gulf of Maine and then down the Maine coast, stopping if necessary in Portland and then on to Cape Ann and into Boston. With luck and good weather I'll do fine. I know I'm in over my head. I would like to wait but I won't or can't. There is something waiting for me in the ring somewhere ahead of me.

There is a going away party at Dewey's house Saturday night. A lot of people are there and many promise to get up early and see me off Monday morning. I hope most of them sleep in. It will be fine if Heather shows up by herself, but that's not likely. She is at the party and for the first time since she handed me the letter we dance. Trying not to watch, Danny sips a beer as he leans against the kitchen wall. It's Saturday night and the hit parade is on the radio. The kitchen is full of people. We slip outside.

"You know," she says, "I'm terrified of you doing this."

"I'll be fine."

"I don't want anything to happen to you."

"I didn't know you cared."

"I care very much." She pauses. "More than you know."

"Then why did you break up with me?"

She looks away over the lawn. In the distance we can see the tide shimmering in the moonlight.

"I care too much and I thought you'd break my heart."

"Well, I haven't, have I?"

She doesn't answer. Instead she kisses me on the cheek and goes back indoors. I'm relieved. Relieved she still cares and surprised how important it is to me. As usual Dewey is right.

There are more people at the wharf than I expected. My mother, tears in her eyes, hugs me. Her sister, Aunt Beth, who I haven't seen in years, has driven down from Saint John to stay with her. She is crying too and tells me to be careful. Mouse tells me to remember him when I'm world champ. Dewey smiles and slaps me on the shoulder.

"I'll miss you, buddy, good luck." His voice is shaky.

Danny shakes my hand, almost formally and says good-luck. He is holding Heather's hand and never lets go. She looks unhappy.

I slip the ropes and push away. As the sloop begins to bob in the chop I look at Heather. For an instant our eyes meet. She is close to tears. I want to go back and hug her, grab her, put her on board. Instead I do the only thing I can — I go inside the wheelhouse and steer the sloop away from Parrsboro. They are all calling, "Good bye" and "Good luck, Duff." A chorus of voices, the people I love.

1 5

WALLY

I can close my eyes and see her. Her blond hair moving with the breeze, framing her beautiful, melancholy face. This morning she had a look of loss. I wonder if I looked the same? Dewey would know. He would see it, so would my mother. The more hours the sloop points south the more I realize we left too much unsaid. I had the opportunity at the party but I let her walk away.

Eventually I put into Spencers Island and make tea. There is nothing I can do until the tide changes. When sailing in the Minas Basin you have to avoid the incoming tide pushing you back up the coast. I sleep and dream of Heather. She's on board wearing a sailor's suit, pulling up the sail, getting us underway. She is looking at me and laughing and very beautiful. When I awake the sun is sinking. It is very still with only the far off cry of a seagull.

My second day I'm making about five knots and the Bay of Fundy is before me. The coastlines on my port and starboard become smaller and less distinct in the wider bay. The sea becomes more active. The *Martha Jane* is a gaff-rigged sloop, its main sail hanging between top and bottom wooden booms. The booms give the sail plenty of stability and she pulls along nicely in the bigger swells. At the end of my second day I'm five miles off Saint John, New Brunswick.

Sailing at night in unfamiliar waters raises a strange mixture in me of excitement and fear. There are different sounds at night. The wind is more hollow, vibrating sails and lines, whipping them into a chant, and at times the aft sail slaps in the darkness, momentarily losing and then catching the wind. Every couple of hours there is a "Gonk" or "Bonk" off in the distance. Sometimes I see a light, but can't tell if it's something on shore or a ship. Sailing at night is lonely and beautiful.

I hear it before I see it. A human sound, low then gradually louder. Every few minutes it comes through the darkness. Is somebody out there, ahead of me? "AHOY! AHOY!" — there is no answer. It's ahead of me off my starboard. Through the next hour the noise comes and goes. Suddenly the moon clears the clouds and soft yellow light brightens the surface of the sea. I can't see anything until I hear it again almost directly in front of me. Shiny, shimmering in the moonlight; mist and water shooting into the air. I can see the spray. We travel together. The whale goes underwater, stays a few minutes, resurfaces, blows, dives again. It's feeding and following the food but my imagination is going wild. The whale is an omen, guiding me along this uncharted path. We're partners. He's up front clearing the way, I'm in the back bringing along the sloop; we're partners moving down the bay. I've seen whales but never anything this size. My guess is it's what they call a right whale. Every time it breaks the water it looks bigger. My partner needs a name. Wally. Wally the whale. At 4 a.m. he dives and doesn't come back. I wait five, ten, fifteen minutes. Wally doesn't resurface.

At ten in the morning a dot appears in the distance. I put my binoculars on it. It's a Greek freighter. Eventually we pass close enough for sailors to wave at me, the first people I've seen in three days. I want the whale to come back.

Off Grand Manan Island I encounter a huge white yacht. There is music and people partying, men and women holding glasses. I trim the sail and go close enough to hear the tinkle of ice. They're from Portland, Maine, going to Yarmouth.

"Come on board and have a drink," one woman calls.

"We love Nova Scotia."

Thanking them I move steadily away.

It's late afternoon when I realize I haven't checked the marine weather. The sky is turning black and it's starting to rain. The weather forecast isn't good. A storm warning has been issued for the Scotia Shelf and the Bay of Fundy. I'm angry with myself for forgetting something so important as the weather. I have to choose: turn back to Grand Manan, go closer to shore and try to find a sheltered harbor or ride out the storm. I don't want to turn back and finding a sheltered cove is too dangerous with dark coming on. The storm isn't a major one, winds of thirty to forty knots. I decide to ride it out. I put on my oil skins and make a thermos of coffee.

An hour later I know I've made a big mistake. The waves have turned into tunnels of water and the wind is howling. I turn on the engine and lower the sails and keep the sloop bow first into the troughs. The *Martha Jane* dives like she's going to the bottom. Water rolls over the deck and the ropes to the mast shake violently. It's turned very dark and I'm scared.

Suddenly we're hit broadside by a wall of water. I don't know where it came from. I went directly into the trough but it hits the *Martha Jane* port side and shakes her so hard it's all I can do to hang on to the wheel. The cans and dishes are crashing in the galley. The remains of lunch, an empty can of Irish stew, is rolling back and forth, clanging and banging as it goes. I'm off course. Hour after hour, water crashes over the wheelhouse. After one violent broadside the sloop shakes and moves backward then pitches down into the darkness. There is a splitting sound and ropes are flying into the windows of the wheelhouse, wildly flying, slapping anything in their path: the mast, the wheelhouse, the deck. I am beside myself with fear. I hang on the wheel as if I were riding some wild animal.

Suddenly I start to shake. Can't stop. Am I having a nervous breakdown? My legs vibrate, my hands hold the wheel while my elbows go back and forth as if I'm trying to fly. The shaking stops and starts again. Things go hazy. I seem to keep waking from a trance. I'm very cold, haven't touched the coffee.

The old man was never one for religion but my mother took me to church. I haven't prayed much, but tonight I pray as I've never prayed before. I ask for everything. Forgiveness for leaving my mother alone. I could have been a better son, I could have been many things.

It is 3:20 in the morning. The water is crashing around me, the ropes are dancing insanely on the deck, the wind is screaming. I'm going to die.

The first sign of dawn is just a slit of rosy light on the horizon. The wind gradually subsides. It's four-thirty when I can finally tie down the wheel and try to secure the flying ropes. The bowsprit is broken, part of it hanging over the side, one of the ropes still attached. I'm incredibly tired, but before anything else I must do something with the bowsprit, the spar extending from the stem of the sloop. It holds the lines steady and gives the main sail stability. I jury-rig a temporary repair job. I have lost track of where I am. I keep falling asleep at the wheel, awake, asleep, awake. Several hours later I find a buoy. By noon I'm sailing up an inlet approaching a coastal community. Rustic warehouses, nets and fishing boats are coming into view. An old man is standing on a wharf watching me. Pipe smoke streams above him as he takes my lines and ties them to iron rings. He walks back to the stern to read my home port, nods and walks back to me.

"You spend the night out there?"

Too tired to reply, I nod. He shakes his head, trying to figure why anybody would be stupid enough to be out in a storm.

"Welcome to Machias."

The people of Machias, Maine, may be the friendliest in the world. In ninety minutes, I've had breakfast, found a place to stay and made arrangements to fix the bowsprit, all courtesy of the old man at the wharf. His name is Emanual Hoffhorn, known by everybody in Machias as Manny.

There isn't much about boats Manny doesn't know. He's working on a new bowsprit for me now as I sit watching him. I'm staying with his neighbor. I had twelve hours sleep and three steaming bowls of fish chowder. I'm still badly shaken, uncertain if I'll ever go back on the water.

Manny has been to sea all his life. He was a cabin boy on a schooner at fourteen and has worked under sail, steam and diesel. He jumps from one story to another so fast I'm never sure where one ends and another begins. He stops often to light his pipe. With full smoke coming out of it, he bends over my new bowsprit and starts again.

"Once sailed with this captain, awful drinker he was, locked himself away in his cabin for five days, crew goin' crazy, didn't know where we was, nobody to take a bearing. First mate so scared of the old man he wouldn't do nothing. So the crew held a meetin' and went and knocked on the old man's door. He looked like hell run over, drunk as a skunk he was, but told us to come in and he listened while we complained about bein' lost and not knowin' where we was. The captain staggers to his chart table and announces we're going to this little island right here off Venezuela — and he points at this little speck. Then one of the crew, old George Simpson, goes over to the chart and flicks the island away with his finger.

" 'That's fly shit, captain.' "

" 'Don't tell me my business,' roars the old man and we all clear out. Next day though he's on deck for his watch and eventually gets us to Maracaibo. Knew his stuff, he did, even if he was drunk half the time. His name was Johnson, Captain William Johnson. After that he was known as Flyshit Johnson. It stuck to him like flyshit for the rest of his life."

Manny's last ship was the S.S. *Duchess of Devon*

"Finest ship you ever saw. I was mate for seven years, all over the world with her. Loved that ship."

Sunday afternoon he takes me in his old truck to meet Captain Douglas Kirkpatrick. Doesn't tell me why except the captain is a friend of his. The captain's house is perched on a hill five miles from Machias. It faces the sea and on his big front porch you can see the rocky coast. I stand and stare at the fabulous view, the water calm and peaceful, a sharp contrast to the fierce sea of a few nights ago.

Captain Kirkpatrick is a weather-beaten wrinkled man, tall and stooped, with brown spots on his hands and face. His eyes are something else, bright, as if to say the mind is still in command. He listens as Manny tells him about my experience in the storm.

"Sailing near the coast, son, is more dangerous than on the open sea. A storm can slap ya down real fast and the rocks can kill ya quicker than a Barbary pirate. You're a lucky lad."

"Captain, when I got to Machias I wasn't sure I'd ever get back on that boat. I'm not sure now."

He smiles and looks off to the water.

"I lost a ship once, my first command. Took charge of her in New York, lost her five months later in the South China Sea. Thought I was finished, thought I was through with the sea."

Then he looks at me.

"You're not through with the sea until it says so. I stayed until I was seventy-two and they wouldn't give me a ship any more."

His doctor advised him not to drink or smoke. He tells me this while serving a second round of rum and puffing on a big cigar. He is seventy-nine and a man who has seen the world. After several wonderful stories of their sailing days and some small talk between him and Manny, he asks me about boxing. Manny has obviously told him about me and I give him some details about myself. I tell him about the club and Moncton and the Cuban. Then he floors me.

"I saw Jack Johnson once, time he lost his title."

"You saw Johnson?" He's got to be pulling my leg. Johnson was one of the great fighters of all time. "But I thought Johnson fought a long, long time ago."

He smiles. "It was a long time ago — 1915 and my second trip to Cuba. Our ship was tied up and a bunch of us went into Havana to see the fight. Hottest day I ever saw, Johnson and Jess Willard fighting outdoors under that sun, round after round. You couldn't believe the heat."

I pepper him with questions. I want to know everything: about the fight, about Johnson, about his stance, his punch, about Willard, how Willard won. He gets up and leaves the verandah, coming back with a framed photograph of a huge black man on his back on the canvas. It's Johnson at the end of his career, one of the most incredible careers in boxing.

"Johnson and Willard were tough beyond words," he says. "The fight went twenty-six rounds. Willard weighed more and was younger but Johnson was the better fighter. Age beat Jack Johnson, age beats us all. Fella at the fight was taking pictures and I bought one on the spot. When our ship got home three months later this photograph was waiting for me."

I realize I've been holding the photo for a long time and pass it back to him.

"You keep it," he says.

"What," I stammer as Manny smiles. "I can't. This, this is worth something. I can't just take it."

"Yes, you can. Rather give it to somebody who wants it than to one of my grandkids who would just break it."

He means it, I can hear it in his voice. I look at the photograph and try to think of something to say. The best I can manage is to mumble, "Thank you, Captain."

Driving back to Machias, Manny tells me about the captain.

"Had a son named Duncan, a pretty fair middleweight back in the thirties. He died suddenly when he was twenty-four, a brain hemorrhage. They never knew if it was boxing but his mother never got over it and she never stopped blaming the captain for bragging up boxing to his son. She left him the next year. We talk every week and when I told him a young Canadian boxer was in Machias he told me to bring you up to the house. He saw something in you, Duff, otherwise he wouldn't have let go of that picture. I know him, he saw something in you."

The next morning we affix the new bowsprit to the *Martha Jane*. Twice I go below deck to look at the Jack Johnson photograph. The old man would have loved it.

16

THE SPY GLASS

I'm staying in a big boardinghouse next to Manny's ramshackle bungalow. The boardinghouse is run by Mrs. Irene MacDonald, known simply as Mrs. Mac. There are three other boarders as well as Mrs. Mac's daughter, Cory.

Cory is in her late twenties, a big blond woman who bosses around her mother, her two dogs and the other boarders. Cory has been married but there is no husband around. She spends her time cleaning the big house. She bowls two nights a week and leaves the cooking to her mother. A wise choice because Mrs. Mac is a great cook. Her stuffed, steamed salmon served with marsh greens and new potatoes is incredible. She pan fries halibut and serves blueberry pancakes for breakfast. I try to be there for the meals. The rest of the time I'm with Manny.

Manny and I give the *Martha Jane* a test run with the new bowsprit. He takes the wheel and the two hour cruise around Machias is one ongoing lecture. I learn more in these hours than in all the books I've read and all the hours Dewey and I spent on the water. Manny devotes a lot of time to talking about the wind. I should have known the storm was coming even without turning on my radio.

"The wind is your gauge. It does more than push your sloop, it tells you what's coming and from where."

He teaches me things I should have known before leaving Parrsboro. The next day we're off on a longer cruise and he talks about the water. How different waves tell you different things. He teaches me how to look at the horizon and what to look for. I take the wheel and he watches me tack.

"Too slow, too slow."

The next day we make improvements to the ropes. The day after that we change the galley so the dishes, pots and pans are more secure.

I have been in Machias over a week and haven't worked out. I worry about staying in shape and mention it to Manny, and from somewhere an old punching bag suddenly hangs from the rafters of his workshop.

I could be living on the sloop instead of at Mrs Mac's. I could be going on my way. Every morning when I wake up I think, tomorrow I'll go, but now I'm in no hurry.

On my ninth day I start to work out in earnest, two hundred sit-ups in the morning, five miles of roadwork in my steel-toed army boots, and then into Manny's shed for a work out with the bag. Then back to Mrs. Mac's for lunch and then sailing with Manny.

Cory begins to have breakfast with me. She's looking better in the mornings, putting on makeup and combing her hair. Maybe she's been sick and just let herself go. I don't ask. I also notice she isn't arguing with her mother as much. Her disposition has improved.

I do my push-ups before breakfast in my room. I'm up to 125 when I see her feet. The door was ajar and Cory pushed it open. I know they're her feet by their shape: fat, thick, wrapped in white sockettes. I just keep going, 130, 131, 132. Ten push-ups later I sneak a peek, hoping she's gone. The sockettes are still there. 140, 141, 142. My shirt is off, I'm naked from the waist up and it's difficult to concentrate when you know somebody is just standing there, watching. Keep going, I tell myself, don't stop. At 191, she breaks the silence.

"God, you have a wonderful body."

Cory, whose real name is Cordeen, has an unappealing voice; a nasal twang turns her words into a whine. Keep going, keep going, keep going —199, 200, 201, 202. At 250 I do what I usually do: ex-

75

tend my arms and, still in the push-up position, slowly count to fifty. It's during this time the sockettes move; flop, flop, flop across the floor they come, two white walruses moving toward me. She is standing over me now and puts a hand on my back, moves it up to my shoulders, then down my back again. I'm frozen, like a man caught in midair. She leans close to my ear and in a raspy whisper says,

"If you want some exercise, Mr. Boxer, I'll go a couple of rounds with you."

She waits for a reply. There isn't any. The walruses are moving again, shuffling, retracting across the floor. She's out the door and I sink to the floor. I haven't drawn a breath in a full minute.

After lunch I tell Mrs. Mac I'm leaving tomorrow. When I tell Manny he simply nods.

"Yep, I guess it's time you got underway."

He takes me up to the small restaurant where he bought me my first meal in Machias. We sit at a corner table and have a couple of beers.

"Manny, I've got a little money. I want to pay you for your time, for the bowsprit, and the sailing lessons. Let me give you something."

"You bought the beer," he says.

"That's not enough."

"More than enough. I enjoyed having you around. Gets lonely here sometimes. Hope you drop in on your way home."

It reminds me of Dewey's question a month ago. "What makes you think I'm going home?"

"Everybody goes home, sooner or later. I went to sea for fifty years but when it was over, where would I go but here, home. I didn't hardly know anybody. Most of the people were gone or dead, but my roots was still here. You'll go home."

I think of Heather and Parrsboro and my leaving the wharf. Home. God, it seems so long ago. I haven't gone very far, yet somehow I feel I've been away for years and traveled the world over. It's hard to explain but I'm not the same person I was on that Monday morning two weeks ago when they all came to say good-bye. To be exact, it was thirteen days ago but it seems like a lifetime. You can travel a long way without going far and you can age a lot in thirteen days.

Mrs. Mac is a sweet woman; she says the way to a man's heart is through his stomach and it didn't take her long to learn lobster is my favorite food. I only told her I was leaving this morning and she's got a lobster supper for me. Before we all sit down, she hugs me and tells me they'll all miss me.

Cory is back to her old self, stains on her dress, shouting at old Mr. Binns, the boarder who has been with Mrs. Mac for twenty-five years.

Mrs. Mac invites Manny to supper. He arrives at exactly six, carrying a package under his arm. He sets it down in the living room and doesn't say anything about it. During the meal, Manny, Mrs. Mac and I do all the talking. Mr. Binns is very deaf and doesn't say much. Mrs. Wiles, another boarder, laughs once in a while and seems to be enjoying herself. Cory eats and looks sulky.

We start off with a huge platter of steamed clams and tiny bowls of melted butter for dipping. Then we have a seafood salad filled with warm scallops. Then two lobsters are placed in front of me. More melted butter. Mrs. Mac offers me another lobster but when I decline she says she'll make me a lobster salad to take on the sloop.

After supper Manny suggests we go for a stroll down to the *Martha Jane*. When we walk onto the wharf he hands me the package. I start to unwrap it.

"No, not now. Wait till you're on the water."

I put the package on my bunk in the sloop and we walk back to Manny's house.

"Well, Manny, I don't know what to say. Thanks for everything."

"You talk like I won't see you again. I'll be there in the morning."

"I'm leaving early, at dawn." The minute it's out of my mouth I realize how silly this sounds. Manny is always up before dawn.

I toss all night, filled with anticipation and something else, maybe fear. When I think of walking down to the wharf and untying the *Martha Jane* my hands sweat.

"I'm afraid," I say out loud in the dark. I shiver. For the first time in days I think of the old man giving one of his lectures on fear, how a real man faces it, beats it down with raw courage.

"Afraid?" his voice mocks me. "Afraid to go on, to step your foot in the ring in the United States of America? Afraid to test yourself?" Now that he's dead, I tell him things I never said before.

"Afraid of the sea?" he asks more tenderly.

"Yes," I reply.

When I finally get to sleep, the old man is swirling through my dreams. One minute I'm in the ring with him and the next it's a naked Cory. She is in the water, swimming ahead of the sloop. She dives, resurfaces, shoots mist into the air and dives again. I am trying to change course, to leave her in the water ahead of me, but the wheel won't move.

With shaky legs I walk onto the wharf at sunrise. Manny is waiting, looking off to the horizon.

"You got a good day." He's set a course allowing me to hop-scotch down the coast.

Manny and I shake hands stiffly and then, much to his embarrassment, I hug him.

"Get away now, before you lose the wind."

My last image of him is exactly the same as my first. He's standing on the wharf, pipe smoke swirling around his head.

An hour later I retrieve his package and open it. My hands shake as I look at it. A brass spy glass inscribed — "To First Mate E. Hoffhorn from the officers & crew SS *Duchess of Devon*."

1 7

MARK, GLORIA
AND A RESCUE

Fear of returning to the water brings the old man back to me.
He's next to me at the wheel of the sloop, going over all our lessons,
all the hours of instruction. When I was eleven we spent that entire
summer on counterpunching. He worked me hard that summer. It's
so difficult to learn to punch back after just being hit yourself. I
couldn't get the hang of it. He'd hit me and expect me to instantly
deliver a counterpunch. All summer it was counterpunching, counterpunching. I hated that summer and hated him for making me do it.
God, I miss him. I can tell myself the truth, boxing isn't the same.
He's not there to push me and pushing, a great deal of pushing, is
what I need right now. I pushed myself back on the water after being
so scared I shook and my breathing turned to gasps. Scared, yes, yet
look at me. I'm back in the sloop, pushing myself into a life that's a
blur, a mystery. I have no idea what the future holds. All I know is
I'm heading for Boston and from there to a gym called Rico's in a
place called Scollay Square. I have no contact, no name, only a gym
that may not even be in business. The old man knew it years ago, in
his days in the navy. When I get there, I'll convince people I can

fight, that I'm capable of becoming a champion, maybe one of the best. Can I do it without him pushing me?

Manny has charted a course that takes me along coastal Maine. My next destination is Bar Harbor. With good weather I'll be there before dark. I told Manny I wanted all daylight sailing. I'm not ready for another night at sea.

I find the buoys and landmarks he's given me and by seven o'clock after a good day on the water I'm anchored off the yacht club in Bar Harbor. The evening is warm and the town crowded; summer tourists fill the restaurants. I walk around looking in store windows and watching people. Finally I buy a hot dog and sit in a park. A band is playing. It is what you would call a tranquil evening.

The wharf at the Bar Harbor yacht club is also crowded. Every size and shape of yacht is tied up. I had to anchor a few hundred yards off shore. Rowing my dingy back to the *Martha Jane* I see a sleek forty-foot, two-masted yacht has glided between my sloop and the shore. The *Martha Jane* is hidden behind its bulk. The name on the stern is *Ocean Lassie* – Providence, Rhode Island. Next to her my sloop looks like a homemade, rough cut wooden boat without the sleek lines, chrome and teak decking. Which of course is exactly what the *Martha Jane* – Parrsboro, Nova Scotia is: rough cut and home-made.

The *Ocean Lassie* is only a few feet from my sloop. A man and woman are sitting on deck having a drink.

"Hallo," he says, walking to the rail as I come aboard the *Martha Jane*. "How you doin'?"

"Fine," I reply.

He holds his hand over the rail.

"Name's Mark Fines. This is my wife Gloria."

We shake hands and they invite me over for a drink.

"I'm in training but maybe some juice or milk would be fine."

"Training, you're an athlete?"

Mark is in the furniture business and obviously successful. The *Ocean Lassie* is beautiful. The sleeping quarters are incredible, there's dark paneled wood everywhere. The Fines give me the grand tour and they're even nice enough to admire the *Martha Jane*.

"Looks like a trusty ship," Mark says, draining his drink. He pours another from an icy pitcher of gin and something. They arrived an hour ago, the first time they've ventured very far from Providence.

"We're celebrating," Mark says.

The three of us sit on their deck and talk sailing. They ask me about Nova Scotia and I tell them about Parrsboro, about buying the sloop and sailing off in the morning with family and friends at dockside. I tell them about the storm and landing in Machias.

"God!" Gloria says, her face a little flushed from the gin. She's an attractive woman with short brown hair. She's older than my first impression, maybe thirty-five or forty. Age lines are eating away at her good looks. There is a hint of a bruise on her cheek which she's tried to conceal with heavy makeup. There are dark circles under her eyes.

He looks younger, fit, ramrod straight, dark hair with a mustache. As the evening wears on they become argumentative, sniping at each other. I think the trip from Providence has frayed their nerves. But I'm so relieved to have put in a day's sailing, to have completed my first day back on the water, that I'm in no hurry to go to bed.

"We've been married fifteen years," says Mark.

"Fourteen," says Gloria.

"Fifteen, isn't it?"

"Fourteen."

It goes on like this. Every detail, every comment is debated and argued over. I finish my milk and excuse myself.

There is no escape. When I go to my bunk, I hear every word and their words are not pretty. An hour later their voices are loud, biting and vulgar.

"Jesus Christ, do you have to argue about every fucking thing," he screams.

"Fuck you and all the people who look like you," she screams back. "You ever get a fucking fact right in your life, it would be a miracle."

"I get enough of them right to keep you in the good life," he roars.

"You call this the good life, living with a fucking shit like you?"

There are people all around them in other boats, people getting fed up. There are courteous comments, first.

"Please be quiet."

The politeness of the yachting fraternity quickly frays and the comments become orders, serious and demanding.

"Shut up, you two."

There is a scuffle. Mark and Gloria are shouting, chairs are over-turning, Gloria is crying, other people now calling in alarm.

"For God's sake, you two, what are you doing?"

"Call the police."

"Let go of me, let go of me," Gloria shrieks.

There is commotion and more abusive language and more calls to call the police. Finally it peters out. There is only the sound of Gloria weeping, her soft moan blending with the light breeze that rattles the lines of the fifty or sixty yachts clustered around us. Far away music is playing. Gloria continues to cry.

I listen to her a long time. It is the most mournful crying, like a lifetime of hurt coming out of her, spilling onto the deck and over the sides into the water. I fall asleep, wake up and listen again. Do I leave her alone or do I go and see if I can help her? What can I do? I can't sleep anyway, maybe I can help.

She's sitting in the same deck chair.

"You okay, Gloria?"

The crying stops.

"Mind your own fucking business." Her voice is low and angry. Her hostility is ugly.

All in all it's pretty good advice, though. At first light I turn on the engine, pull anchor and leave Bar Harbor. I look back once and she is watching me. We don't wave good-bye.

I have a very full day ahead headed for Boothbay Harbor. I'm two hours out of Bar Harbor, sailing under a sky not totally cleared of darkness, when a flare goes up off my port bow. "Damn it." A new fear grips me. I want to ignore it, pretend I don't see it. I tell myself, it's too far away, but it isn't. There is no choice, it's the law of the sea: I have to respond. "Somebody's life," I tell myself. "Somebody's life." I turn my engine on and change course. Five minutes later another flare lights up the sky in front of me. Twenty minutes later I bear down on a thirty-eight foot fishing boat with three figures silhouetted in the ocean dawn. The *Nancy J.* is out of Gloucester. Coming back from the Scotia Shelf, she started taking water. It might have something to do with the her load. She's so full of fish she's practically down to her gunnels.

The three crew members are young, two of them rosy-faced boys under woollen caps. Two of them jump on board with a towline. They're brothers, the oldest might be twenty. He talks in a series of short sentences, as if he's having a conversation with himself, answering questions before I ask them.

"Name's Butch, I'm skipper, these my brothers, damned if I know, things great one minute and water pouring in the next. You tow us. We got a pump going but the engine room is flooded. How big an engine you got?" He is in constant motion, securing the towline as he talks.

"Where to?" I ask.

"Get us to Swan Island. We'll call Gloucester and Dad will bring another boat and some caulking and pitch."

The *Martha Jane's* engine is throbbing under the strain of towing the bigger boat. Our progress in slow. For four hours and forty minutes we're on a nail biting ride as the towrope stretches to its limit. If it breaks, Butch says we'll circle round and put another one on. He and his brothers are running their pump as fast as possible. Even so the *Nancy J.* is getting lower and lower in the water. I'm running the engine at full throttle. My stomach is in knots. If the brothers are concerned, they're hiding it better than I am.

"That towrope is so taut you could play a tune on her," says Donald, two years younger than Butch. He slaps me on the back.

"Glad you came along, mate, we was gettin' jumpy out there." The youngest brother is Malcolm. He's seventeen and tells me they have a cottage and boathouse on the island. There is a lighthouse equipped with a ship to shore radio. "Our ship to shore died the third day we was out. Donald tried to get it going, but no luck."

Swan Island is finally a tiny speck in the distance. Gradually its gray rocks and spindly evergreens get bigger. My engine throbs and the gas pump on the fishing boat contributes to the drama. Will it hold out just a little longer? The brothers watch the towline and smoke cigarettes while leaning against the wheelhouse. We all talk, often at the same time, excited and bonded by this high seas adventure.

When we arrive they waste no time. An old truck hauls the *Nancy J.* on a skid right out of the water. Butch is back and forth giving orders and securing things. The first job is transferring the catch and getting it to Gloucester. They are experienced in the many necessary tasks. One of them is putting extra fuel in my tank.

"Can't thank you enough," Butch says and hands me a cheque.

"This isn't necessary," I say.

"No, take it."

It's a company cheque from Jansen Sea Foods, Gloucester, for one hundred dollars.

"That's our family business. You saved our catch and maybe us. You don't get nothing for saving our skins." He smiles. "This is for taking you off course, out of your way."

By mid-afternoon I'm several knots south of Swan Island with a new sense of myself. The old man would be proud of me. "Don't get cocky," he would say. Then I think of Gloria, sitting there before daybreak this morning, looking so mournful and beaten. Looking over the water, I think of Wally, and wonder where that whale is, right now.

18

GLOUCESTER

Through a variety of weather, I gradually make my way down the coast. The engine has been going a lot. I fill up in South Portland then face a day of rain and no wind and have the engine going again. When I reach Massachusetts, the coast changes with less of the rocky inlets and islands. I'm off Manny's schedule and spend two nights anchored in little unmarked inlets. The first night is fine, I have a good sleep and cook a big breakfast. Three nights later when I try the same type of shelter, a stiff breeze keeps dragging the *Martha Jane* closer to shore and I have to haul anchor and take the sloop farther out. Then I'm too far away from shore and almost get run over by a tanker. It's one of those nights when nothing goes right.

Suddenly in mid-afternoon the sail is full and I don't have to tack back and forth. I'm going to bypass Manny's plan and stay with the wind as long as possible. This is a big decision. I'm back on the water at night. This time I've listened to the weather forecast on my marine radio and this time I have the notes I made of Manny's instruction on the wind. I watch the talltales, little pieces of cloth attached to the sail, looking for any change. The moon is bright and the wind continues and once, just once, I think I hear the whale. By morning I'm within a few knots of Gloucester.

I'm finishing lunch in a small restaurant near the Gloucester waterfront when who walks in but Butch and Donald. We greet each other with slaps and vigorous handshakes as buddies do who have shared a common experience and faced danger together.

"Malcolm is still up on Swan Island. We got the fish here. He's recaulking the *Nancy J.* Then they're going to pitch her and bring her back."

Over coffee Butch suggests I come over and meet his father.

"Dad would like to meet you for sure."

Max Jansen is a bald, round-faced man of about sixty who, if he had a white beard, would make a perfect Santa Claus. He grips my hand.

"What a pleasure, Mr. Martin."

"Just call me Duff."

"I owe you for saving my boys and the catch. How long are you staying in Gloucester?"

"Until morning."

"Have dinner with us then. Let us treat you to a real New England meal."

We agree to meet at a place called Neptune's.

Max and his sons meet me in the bar. We take a table by a window overlooking fishing boats. The sun is beginning to set and the water is a rosy glow. They have wine and I drink orange juice. We talk about boats and boxing and where I'm going.

"You know Boston, Mr. Jansen?"

"Max will do just fine and to answer your question, a little bit, mostly the waterfront."

"Ever hear of a place called Rico's?"

"Can't say that I have. We go to North Station to watch the Bruins sometimes, but I don't follow boxing."

The conversation drifts — government, the difference between Canada and the States. Max and his sons are Republicans.

"I've never voted Democrat and never will."

Over fried clams, salad and baked haddock Max tells me the incident off Swan Island has changed things for his family. "A watershed of sorts, I guess, and, Duff, you're part of it." He leans across the table, taking full command of the conversation.

"We take things so casually, and just ignore the circumstances. What if, just suppose, you hadn't come along and the *Nancy J.* sank. I'm not saying the boys would have drowned. They had a dory but they would have been bouncing about in a lot of water in a little open boat."

He looks at me hard.

"It could have been bad, very bad, so we had a family meeting and decided from now on three brothers don't go anywhere in the same boat. My wife's dead and these boys are all I got."

He stares me right in the eye.

"I don't know if you're a religious man, if you believe in fate, if you believe things are planned out by a higher power, but I do and I believe it was planned that you were where you were. It's all planned for us." There is silence and it gets a little awkward until Butch gently punches his father's shoulder.

"If anyone can bring talk to a stop it's Max Jansen."

We laugh and the conversation turns to sports.

On the walk back to the *Martha Jane* Butch and Donald elaborate on the family meeting. They had never seen their father so serious.

"We didn't have much say in the matter. It wasn't so much a family meeting as Max just getting us all together and telling us," Donald says. "I mean, I see his point but it's the kind of rule that only people with more than one boat can afford to follow."

Donald is eighteen but he talks with the maturity of a much older person.

"It's a big change for us because when the company was starting and we were little kids, we all went out with him. Dad and his three sons all in the same boat. People here do that all the time. The thing is, he's getting old and he worries more. Didn't worry when he was our age. Now he's got money and he worries. Is that what getting old and getting wealthy does to you?"

The fore and aft sails are full, and the *Martha Jane* is clipping through the water south of Gloucester. Max's words are running through my mind. His comments on higher power hang onto me. I try the concept on other things, love for example: if things are planned out, what does that mean in love? Were Heather and I destined to break up? Was the old man supposed to die and leave me when he did? I've had a dozen fights in the last three years and won them all. Is all that planned by some higher power? Boston is only a few hours away now, the sea is calm with light winds. Standing at the wheel I hear Max saying, "It's all planned for us."

A steady stream of ships are off in the distance — freighters, tankers and tugs. Harbor traffic headed for Boston. A couple of dozen noisy seagulls suddenly surround me, looking for food. Their white runny droppings hit the wheelhouse window. A nautical greeting. "Welcome to Boston, Duff. You made it."

19

LENNOX LEMAY

Boston is big. I've never seen such a busy harbor. It takes me a long time to find a place to tie up. I'm chased away from a fishery wharf and go along for forty-five minutes and try another place by a cannery, but I'm told I can't stay there either. Finally, I find a place by an old freight wharf. After the sloop is secure I start walking. Don't know where, I just start going, taking note of streets so I can find my way back.

I spend the next couple of days getting my bearings, taking walks farther and farther from the waterfront. Eventually I find Scollay Square with its dark, narrow streets and ramshackle buildings. Then I'm at the front of Rico's Gym. It's more dilapidated than I expect, and certainly doesn't look the way the old man so often described it. Below a battered sign is a dirty and cracked glass door with a dark staircase leading up to the second floor. As I climb the stairs I hear a familiar sound. The rat-a-tat rocking hum of someone working a light bag. The gym is big and dark. Peeling paint on pock-marked walls, phone numbers written in pencil. The sun shines through dirty windows, revealing two empty boxing rings. Eight heavy punching bags hang still. The only sound is the rat-a-tat whirl of the light bag.

An old black man is working the bag. He doesn't stop as I walk around looking for somebody in charge. The place seems deserted except for the two of us. The smell of stale perspiration hangs in the air. The Parrsboro Boxing Club never smelled like this.

After a few minutes he stops. He's wearing a blue sweatshirt and gray flannel slacks. His arms are long and he looks in good shape despite his age. He picks up a towel and rubs it vigorously over his face.

"You lookin' for something?" He says the words without looking at me. He's maybe sixty, and has boxed; his nose and ears show it.

"Some information maybe," I say.

"Yeah, like what?"

"Well," is all I manage. What do I want anyway? What am I doing here? There is only one thing to do so I surge ahead, trying to sound calm.

"Well, I'm new in town, hoped I could make some money fighting."

There is silence except for the small punching bag slowly rocking back and forth. He stares at me and I'm startled as he suddenly shrieks. He doubles over in laughter and slaps both knees.

"You gotta be shittin' me?" He points at me. "You with that pretty face, don't look like you ever took a good jab in yo' life." He is moving toward me now and turning very serious. "God Almighty son, club fightin' — dis 'bout gone in dis town. Nobody fightin' in Boston."

I try not to look astonished.

"Philly or New York only places with purses these days. Only thing here is Brighton and they scrape a kid like you off the pavement. You got no business lookin' for fightin'."

He shuffles away, having done his inspection, passed his judgment and written me off as a baby-faced nobody.

"Go home, kid. Get a job that ain't fightin'." He vanishes through a door.

"Can't go home!" I yell at the door he disappeared through. There is no reply. I follow him.

The door leads into a tiny cluttered office. He is already sitting behind a desk.

"Ya runnin' from the law?" he asks.

This makes me laugh but he doesn't crack a smile so I stop.

"I'm not running from anything. I'm trying to get a couple of fights so I can make some money."

He gives me the strangest look, a hard mysterious stare, as if he's witnessing some amazing thing standing in front of him. The look slowly changes to complete and utter sadness as if he's about to cry.

"Kid, fighters don't make no money. Even those who can fight, which you definitely can't. I can tell that by lookin' at ya. You're peanut butter and yams; to fight you gotta be hard rocks and cabbage."

"I can fight, mister. Just tell me where to go."

"I am tellin' ya. Go home and save yourself a lot of grief."

"I've already had a lot of grief," I say and turn to leave.

"Want a drink?" he offers.

His name is Lennox LeMay and in his day he was a respectable middleweight. He touched the big time twenty years ago, which means he isn't nearly as old as he looks. He had challenged the challenger. He'd lost in a good fight. His manager ran out on him, left him broke and he'd managed to stay that way.

"I been here these past eleven years. When we was busy I sparred with a lot of big name fighters, but she's over."

"What happened?" I blurt out, feeling the effects of a glass of bourbon on an empty stomach.

"Football, basketball, other things to do, and now this new television. Folks don't go to club fights no more. They can see the World Series on TV, Marciano fight on television. Why go see some second-rate fighter in a club?"

He shifts in his chair. The office is heavy with the smell of bourbon and old paper.

"When you fight clubs these days, kid, you're fightin' on the bottom of the barrel. Old dogs and bums that's going nowhere, guys you don't wanna mix with."

The booze loosens my tongue and I start to talk. I tell him about the Parrsboro Boxing Club, the old man, my fights, my sloop. He doesn't move, doesn't flinch. Lennox LeMay is a good listener.

Fortified with bourbon I press him. He's skeptical but finally agrees to give me a look. A guy by the name of Cutter is coming in tomorrow and he'll spar with me.

I've been at Rico's most of the afternoon and when I hit the hot summer sidewalks my head is spinning. I'm always in training, seldom drink and I've never had bourbon before. I'm intoxicated, unsteady, and lost. The sun is setting when I finally get back to the sloop. I put my head down and sleep for ten hours.

Cutter is a big man. He's got a flat nose and a barrel chest and I bet he weighs twenty pounds more than me. I've brought my duffel bag and gloves and Lennox tapes my hands. The most pressing question I have is how Cutter got his name. Lennox looks up and smiles.

"He works in a butcher shop. He's a meat cutter. Why, you worried already?"

There are two other men in the gym. They're wearing suits, one wears a fedora. They stay at the far end, leaning against the wall as if they're waiting for something.

"Who are those guys?" I ask Lennox.

"They work for Victor."

"Who's Victor?"

"Victor owns this place and the Brighton Boxing Club."

He gives me this sad look and says, "They're here to see Cutter. There are two guys going to spar with Cutter today. I'm throwing you in first so you can get whipped and get your ass back to Canada."

A minute later the door opens and two young guys come in carrying sports bags. Both are tough looking, as if they've been badly beaten. One of them has a misshapen ear. They speak to Lennox and Cutter and walk into the changing rooms.

Cutter is fast. He's got a strong right jab and he uses it quickly on me four times. I'm just staying out of his way, adjusting to being back in the ring. I feel out of my element. The old man's voice is inside me, telling me Cutter's jab is not invincible. He isn't using his left hand enough and carries it a little low. Cutter comes at me with another jab and I hit him with a right cross. He stops and I hit him again with sharp jabs, one two, three. I'm loosening up. I throw a good left hook. It hammers him hard right on the jaw. He wavers but maintains his balance and glares at me. Too bad for him. I hit him with another jab then another left hook. I've taken over the fight. The last hook takes his breath away. Lennox is watching and the two guys in suits move closer to the ring. Cutter throws a right but he's lost his edge.

The old man always said a good boxer knows when to take advantage. I'm back into him with another left jab and another and another. My fists are flying. I swing hard, pushing with my legs and hit him with a right hook. This time his knees have gone to mush. He tilts and topples. As he hits the canvas, he groans.

There is silence, absolute silence. Cutter, with bleary eyes, is looking up at Lennox, who leans against the ropes, staring at Cutter. Cutter doesn't attempt to get up. Except for our heavy breathing you could hear a pin drop. It's like a time warp, things seem suspended. I have no idea what to say.

Finally one of the suits hauls himself up to the ring. He's the one without the fedora, a small man, natty dresser, cream suit and green tie.

"Good punching, kid, my name's Jimmy Demato. How long ya been boxin'?"

I give him a short version of my career while he lights a cigar.

"Want you to come up to Victor's with us. We might have a spot for you."

"When?" I reply.

"Right now."

Cutter gets himself up.

"What about me, Mr. Demato?"

"Later, Cutter."

2 0

V I C T O R

I sit in the back seat. Jimmy does the driving and the other guy does the talking. His name is Gus Russo. He's maybe fifty, a brute, big frame and a flat face, looks like he might have been a boxer. The noticeable thing about Gus is his hands; he has huge hands. He asks me the usual stuff, where I'm from and how long I've been in Boston. Minutes pass without a word. Then Gus makes a half turn from the front seat and says, "Listen, kid, I want you to know something about Victor. He don't like smartasses, okay? Just do what he says and don't be givin' him any backtalk. I know you won't anyway, 'cause you're not that kind of guy. But I'm just telling you, Victor don't like backtalk, okay?"

"Sure," I say, feeling just a little uncomfortable.

"Yeah," Jimmy chimes in, "today is not the day to piss off Victor." Gus looks at him. Although I can only see his profile, I see enough to know Gus is giving Jimmy a steely, ice-cold look.

My buoyant spirits are leveling out as we reach the Brighton Boxing Club. It's a big white wooden building standing alone. Although it's early afternoon on a working day the parking lot is half full. When we go through the door it's like entering another world, from daylight to spotlight. The first thing I see is a girl dancing on a stage. She isn't wearing much clothing and is removing what she is

94

wearing. Guys cheer her on. We pass a long bar with three or four bartenders washing glasses and arguing over a ball game. We pass tables where people are playing cards. A lot of the men are older guys and a lot of the women have bleached blond hair. We walk through the noise and commotion of card games and girls and ice in glasses. A hundred different sounds above the music and the stripper. "Come here, come here," a white-haired man yells at a woman who is quickly walking away from his table, amidst hoots and laughter from the other card players. As we pass tables, Gus and Jimmy often speak to people but don't stop. There is plenty of money on the tables but the games seem different. At some tables people are practically jumping up and down, making a big commotion. At others tables they don't move or make a sound, as if they're in deep concentration. I have never seen a place like this.

We head to the far corner, where a crowd stands watching something. As we approach with Jimmy in the lead, people separate to make a path for us. We walk up to a card game with an incredible amount of money on the table, must be thousands of dollars. With his back to the wall sits a little old man. He's wizened, at least seventy, with receding gray hair combed straight back, revealing a severe widow's peak. A big curved nose is the only part of his face that isn't wrinkled but it's his eyes that catch you. They are a contradiction: glassy, lifeless, like a dead man's, yet able to see into you. Immediately I know this is Victor and he is a man treated with deference.

It's Gus who does the talking. "Vic, this kid is a fighter from Canada. He went up against Cutter this morning and made mincemeat out of him. This kid can punch way better than Cutter. Thought maybe you want to put him up against somebody. Maybe we should use him Saturday night instead of Cutter."

Victor looks at me, not friendly at all, a sharp, fierce glare then he goes back to his cards. All eyes are on him waiting for him to say something. When he speaks his voice is thin and raspy. "He's a middleweight, Gussie, not in Cutter's division. Who you got in mind for him?"

"Mario maybe," Gus says, faltering a little.

Victor looks at me again with the eyes of a viper, a look that sends shivers down my back.

"How good are you, kid?"

"Very good."

"How many fights you won?"

"Won them all."

I'm not being smart, but he gives me an even meaner look. He turns his eyes on Gus.

"I don't need to look at him, Gussie, I take your word for it. You say he can fight, he can fight. I'll see him Saturday night. You explain things to him."

He goes back to his game. The interview is over.

Gus grabs my arm and we start to move.

"Nice meeting you, sir."

"Come on." Jimmy pushes me from behind.

"I've put myself on the line for you, kid, don't let me down," Gus says and suggests we have something to eat. The three of us sit at the bar. The girl has finished dancing and the music has stopped. We order club sandwiches and Gus fills me in on Saturday night. I'm fighting this guy Mario. I can train the rest of the week at Rico's since Victor owns the place.

After lunch, still sitting at the bar, I sign a one-page contract. If I win I get two hundred dollars. If I lose I get twenty-five. I ask about a license to fight in Massachusetts but Gus says they'll take care of that. I ask about a medical and Gus says that will be looked after too.

"We'll look after all the little things; you look after you. No telling where you can go, with us. Victor owns a place in Jersey. They get some big fight cards. No reason we couldn't see you fighting there. Main thing is do what you're told. Victor gets real mad when people don't do as he wants."

I don't understand how they can do a medical without me, but I don't ask. I just want to fight well.

I ask Gus if he's ever been a fighter.

"Not in the ring," Jimmy laughs but doesn't add anything and neither does Gus. Suddenly the music starts and another girl comes on stage. No, it's the same girl in a different outfit and she starts stripping again.

"That broad can grind," Jimmy says. The only thing I know about grinding has to do with coffee but I don't think he's telling me she makes great coffee. Although guys yell things like "Take it off," they really don't pay any attention to her. Only the three of us sitting at the bar look at her.

"She got a face like a dog," Gus snorts. She looks at him and smiles. "Stupid bitch," he growls.

Gus and Jimmy use a lot of words I never heard before; their conversation is peppered with smack, swack, gutso, whacker and piss-head.

"You got a polly, kid?" Jimmy asks.

"A what?"

"A polly, a girlfriend."

"No, not any more."

"You win some big time fights the broads will be all over you." Jimmy winks at me.

"Broads," Gus hisses. "You're better off without them."

It's four o'clock when they drop me off at Rico's so I can make arrangements with Lennox. He's alone in his office. I sit down and tell him of the day's events and that I'm fighting Saturday night at the Brighton Boxing Club, going up against an Italian by the name of Mario. He's giving me that sad look of his and shakes his head.

"Mario's a guy they hope to bring along."

"That's good, isn't it?"

"Not for you, it ain't, not at all."

"Well, they're going to bring me along too."

He looks at me and slowly shakes his head.

"Did you sign a contract?"

"Yeah, why?"

He sighs. "These guys ain't your friends from, what's that place called?"

"Parrsboro."

"Yeah, Parrsboro. These ain't your friends from Parrsboro. You can't mess with these guys, kid."

"They're okay. Jimmy and Gus are okay."

"You think so, you think Gus Russo is okay, do you?" He gets up and starts out of his office then turns to me.

"Kid, Gus Russo is a killer. He kills people who double-cross Victor Delgato. He's Victor's hired killer."

I take a long time getting back to the sloop. My spirits have soared and fallen in a matter of hours. There is a notice tacked to the rail of the *Martha Jane* when I finally arrive. "Move this boat, immediately."

21

ORDERS FROM GUS

I get up the next morning determined. Even if Lennox is right, once they see me fight I'll earn their respect. If I'm good enough I won't have to hang out with hoodlums.

I lace up the steel-toed army boots and start running along the Boston docks, past stevedores covered in flour. Men grunting, trucks and cranes moving — the noise of a busy seaport is exactly what you'd expect.

It takes most of the morning to find another berth for the sloop so it's noon when I get to Rico's. Lennox is alone. I work the light bag then skip for half an hour and put some heavy punches on the big bag. Mid-afternoon a guy named Reggie comes in, and Lennox gets him to spar with me. Reggie isn't particularly fast but I make some sloppy mistakes and he gets in some good shots. We go several rounds with Lennox watching when Jimmy and Gus come in.

We're both winded. My legs feel the strain when Reggie makes a big mistake. He tries to counterpunch but he's sloppy and I give him a good left. It jars him, a slight stagger as his head recoils. Lennox says that's enough. Gus looks angry or upset.

Lennox gets Reggie some ice and holds a towel to his face. His nose is bleeding. My legs feel the strain of several rounds. I tell Lennox.

"I better work the legs the rest of the week."

"Oh, kid," Gus says. "Let's talk a minute." He takes me out of earshot.

"Listen, kid, Victor has been talking to me this morning. He's not happy. He's worried maybe you're too good, ya know," he laughs and taps me on the shoulder. "Don't be too good, okay. I seen you yesterday and I think you're pretty good but I don't think you can beat Mario. I mean, nothin' personal, kid, but you're real young and Mario is goin' places. We got plans for him. So don't kill, know what I mean, don't kill yourself gettin' ready for Saturday."

"I'm still fighting Saturday, aren't I?"

"Oh yeah, you're fightin', but Victor's kinda bringing Mario along — you know, wants to guide him for a few fights, and he's going to squeeze my balls over you, know what I mean, don't kill yourself."

"I'm sorry, Gus, I don't understand. What do you mean, don't kill myself?"

"Jesus, kid, I gotta spell it out. You get your two hundred dollars so don't worry. Just take it easy on Mario 'cause we want him to take a few. Let him get his feet under him, ya see."

"You mean you want me to throw the fight!" I'm getting furious even if he is a goddamn killer.

"We don't call it nothin' like that," he almost shouts, shaking his big head. Gus isn't used to spelling things out; in his world deals are done by inference. He points his finger at me.

"In round five you take a good one. Don't just faint, know what I mean."

"Gus, I can't do that. You got the wrong guy, I can't do that."

"Listen, kid, you're gettin' your money plus a hundred bucks bonus and we're setting you up for two big fights. I seen your stuff. We'll take you to Jersey, four or five hundred bucks a pop. That's why I took you to Victor. You can handle some big fights, you can maybe go up the ranks. You're fast, you got lots of time. Just let Mario win this one. Show us you're with us."

Gus comes close. Still pointing his finger he now presses it on my chest.

"That's the way it is, just this once. Don't piss off Victor, he's got a temper."

He walks away, leaves me there, my head spinning. Lennox and Jimmy are watching. Gus walks up to them, says something, Jimmy waves to me and they're out the door.

I feel sick. My old man told me about throwing fights. He loved boxing for the skill, for the competition, one man against another. Throwing a fight disgusted him. He had his principles. Things were black or white with him and stories of boxers throwing a fight were told to me in a voice of disdain.

Slowly I change into my clothes, pack my duffel bag and without a word to Lennox I leave the gym.

"See you tomorrow," Lennox says. He warned me.

Outside Jimmy is leaning against their black car. He is alone. He puts an arm around me.

"Come on, Duff, it's not that bad, one fight and you won't have to do it again. Think of it as a test, you prove to us you're with us all the way and we'll show you total respect, the respect you deserve. We'll bring you along, give you good fights, let you go up through the ranks. But you know, you gotta pay your dues. Victor extracts a toll for his services, but once you're on Victor's side, once you prove yourself to him, nobody can hurt you." We shake hands and I decline a ride. I need air.

Walking back to the *Martha Jane*, I notice Scollay Square as if I'm seeing it for the first time. Dark little bars, Pabst Blue Ribbon signs. A black and white photograph of Rocky Marciano in a dirty window of a bar with a battered exterior and an electric Budweiser sign with the "w" and "e" missing. The neighborhood is filled with aging shops, little wooden places, narrow side streets where barbers cut hair with their front doors open and old men read newspapers sitting in the sun. The sidewalks are uneven with ends poking up ready to trip you. A butcher shop has choice cuts in the window, sawdust and blood on the floor. A fat butcher in a white coat sweeps the sidewalk and whistles.

An old couple pass me, speaking a language I've never heard before. A few blocks later a man comes out of an alley doing up the buttons on his fly. He looks strange and angry and he stares at me as if I've done something to him. These are the same streets I walked

100

yesterday. Today they are different, shabbier and seem much more dangerous.

When I reach the *Martha Jane* I crawl in my bunk and close my eyes. It's the old man who has betrayed me. All his stories of boxing in Boston. Why didn't he tell me the rest of it? He didn't know the rest of it, I argue, that's why. Who was he to know, a young sailor, dumb and filled with hero worship. Face it, your old man was a blowhard and you bought all his stories, swallowed them, hook, line and sinker. When I start thinking badly of the old man, I really beat myself up. And I'm doing it more often.

For a long time I stay very still in my bunk, listening to the light wind tossing water against the hull, lap, ba-lap lap, ba-lap. I just listen and think. At midnight I raise the anchor, slip the lines and glide out of Boston Harbor.

22

RUNNING

I point the *Martha Jane* to the open sea. The old man's voice is inside my head, giving me shit. He would have stayed and fought and taken Mario and shown the world and suffered the consequences. He would have shown them all the great Alex Martin didn't throw a fight and didn't run.

Outside the harbor the wind is stronger. I sit at the wheel, letting things sweep through my mind. The motion and moon revitalize me. I've got the Big Dipper and can navigate as I look for lighthouses along the coast. The *Martha Jane*'s sail is full, pulling the sloop along at a good speed. I tie myself to the chair and nod off, wake up and nod off again. I have to sail far enough east to round Cape Cod then I'm heading south to New York. The charts are showing shoals and I tack farther off shore. I sail all night and all day, staying at the wheel but napping when I can.

I'm having long arguments with my old man, analyzing his take on all this. I'm doing the only thing I can do. I'm reluctant about New York. It's too close to Boston where I signed a contract with a man who employs killers.

"God! What am I doing?"

Sailing along the coast of Massachusetts I have never felt so alone. I'm nineteen years old, I can take a punch. I'm also weak and it's the weakness I feel now. I'm not living up to expectations. Whose expectations exactly I'm not certain. Are they mine or his? The guilt of running is strong, the sense of failure is overpowering. Tears run down my face. First silent whimpering, then shallow crying, wiping away a tear or two, then bawling, all out crying like I haven't cried since I was three.

That's why I don't see or hear them until they're on top of me. Fifty feet off my port when they let go with their air horn. "United States Coast Guard."

I'm crying like a baby and here's the goddamn coast guard. "Oh shit."

I trim the sail as the cutter comes alongside. Uniformed officers are standing by.

"Coming aboard." It's almost a question, as if I answered, "No thanks, not today," they'd reply, "Oh, sorry," and leave.

He's not much older than me, on my deck now holding out his hand. "Lieutenant Jeff Chalmers. How are you?"

He's looking at my eyes as we shake hands. All I can say is "Duff" and point to my eyes: "Allergies."

He looks doubtful but says nothing. He already knows the sloop is from Nova Scotia. It's written on the stern.

"You're a long way from home. Where you going?"

"New York," I say.

"Pleasure trip?" he asks.

"Yes," I answer as the wild thought crosses my mind that Victor might hear of this encounter — these guys might even pass along information for cash to the underworld. He gives me an official look as two other officers go below deck.

"You carrying anything?" he asks.

"Like what?"

"Contraband," he replies.

I have no idea what contraband is.

"Such as?"

"Alcohol," he replies.

"Couple of beer, want one?"

He thinks I'm being smart, but I'm not. Despite the embarrassment of red eyes I'm glad to have company. Now they're here I want them to hang around.

He gives me a cold look and snaps, "No thanks."

What is he thinking? A lone sailor in a little sloop, hundreds of miles from home, crying like crazy. What the hell's with this guy? I imagine they'll sit around the coast guard lounge somewhere tonight and talk about me, water weirdo of the day.

The two uniforms return to the deck and give Jeff a nod.

"You need bearings or anything, fresh water?"

"I'm fine," I say. "I wasn't trying to be a jerk about the beer. It was an honest offer."

He simply nods and they're gone.

As they disappear, I hate myself all over again. I am the world's biggest dolt. First for trying this, taking this little sloop away from Nova Scotia, for getting involved with hoods in Boston, for being caught crying, for offering a beer to a coast guard officer involved in a vessel inspection.

"God, I'm stupid!" I scream into the wind and immediately I feel better.

I'm not going to New York. I worry about Victor's long reach. I sail off the coast another day and night past Providence, Rhode Island. The weather has been fair but I can't sleep because of the traffic. Bulk carriers and freighters are cutting across my bow. New York is in there to my right and heavy traffic is headed for the Hudson or docks on the East River. I have to stay awake. Big ships can swamp me. If there is absolutely nothing in sight I put my head down and sleep for two or three minutes. It keeps me going through the night.

I'm heading for Philadelphia. Which means hitting the mouth of Delaware Bay and sailing up to Wilmington, then into the Delaware River to Philadelphia. I have no name or contact, but what did I have in Boston? The old man bragged about Rico's and look where that landed me. Philadelphia can't be worse.

It starts to rain. I put on my slicker and stand at the wheel, plotting my future. This time I'm going to find a reputable promoter, get an out-of-state license and not drop in on local gyms babbling about wanting to fight. This time I'll be smarter; Boston has taught me.

The wind comes up and it rains for six hours. When it clears I have no choice — I drop anchor, tie the wheel down and go below. I sleep three hours and when I come back on deck the sun is coming up and there is nothing but ocean in all directions. The sunrise creates a huge highway of red, pink and yellow on the water. It's beautiful.

Two more days and I'm not making good time, just off New Jersey, a hundred miles north of Atlantic City right now. There is little wind and my food is running low except for canned Irish stew. I left Boston without provisions but stew is stew and people live on worse.

I need a good clear night to take bearings, although there is little likelihood I can miss the mouth of Delaware Bay. It's wide and well-marked. Two more days and one clear night and I get my bearings. I change tack and move closer to shore. It's warm and misty.

At eleven o'clock I hear a horn. It's got to be the lighthouse at Cape May at the head of the bay.

Three hours later I'm turning up Delaware Bay. It's raining hard again but I can see the lighthouse and I've gone around buoy number two.

It's really coming down and there is no wind. I drop the sail and turn on the engine. If I can find a little inlet I'll drop anchor.

The rain is making a lot of noise, beating off the windows of the wheelhouse. Drops hit the deck so hard they bounce. Maybe that's why I don't hear him until he's right on top of me. It's just a dull noise, then a different cadence. I stare into the black off the stern. Suddenly I see bow lights bearing down on me, twenty feet away. My running lights are on but it doesn't see me. I jump up and down yelling at the top of my voice. Ten feet away now, coming through the rain is a tugboat.

At the last minute it pulls hard starboard but it's too late. There is a grinding impact that knocks me on the deck. Sprawled on my stomach I get to my hands and knees and scramble to the bow. The initial blow is followed by a deep thud and then a shudder goes through the *Martha Jane* as if the sloop is having a convulsion. Finally, a terrible tearing sound of wood splitting.

There is yelling and cursing, as the tug's engine is thrown in reverse, pulling away. Disconnecting causes more splitting and tearing and the sloop slides sideways. The tug moves alongside, parallel to me now, and someone is yelling.

"Are you okay?" a rough voice calls through the rain.

I get off my knees, dizzy and wet, trying to catch my breath.

"Yeah," is all I can manage. The deck is taking a steeper slope.

"Get off, she's sinking."

What! Sinking! God, no! The bow is lifting!

I scramble below deck and grab my money and duffel bag. The planking is split and water is pouring into the aft. I rush out onto the slippery, tilting deck. It is difficult to keep my footing. Then I remember. I can't leave without them and I fight the incline to go below again. The water is already up to my knees. It's so cold I shudder. I grab Manny's spy glass and the photograph of Jack Johnson. The tug is hard alongside, the captain is frantic as I jump. Another escape. First Parrsboro, then Boston and now the *Martha Jane*. Oh, God, what am I doing?

My poor little sloop is going into the dark water in front of me. Everything is hurtling through me, speeding past my eyes — boxing, the old man, the club, Heather, Dewey, Curly, my mother, Manny, that god-awful sea in Maine, Victor's eyes, Gus's hands, Lennox's sad look, Cutter on the canvas, the whale, that beautiful golden light on the water.

There is the voice again. He calls me to the wheelhouse where it's remarkably warm with the smell of oil and coffee. He's a little old man, alone and sorry. His weather-beaten face shows a lifetime at sea. He has such a strong accent I cannot understand much of what he says. He may be taking on water himself, he says, and can't stick around.

Hours later we end up at the port of Salem near the head of Delaware Bay. There are marine insurance forms, coast guard reports. The tug captain gives the coast guard the bearing where we rammed. They radio a cutter but they can find no sign of the *Martha Jane*.

I have no insurance. Neither does the tug, although working tugs are supposed to carry marine insurance. The tug is damaged but not extensively. The captain keeps talking and talking and talking. He talks through reports and interviews. The coast guard tells me I'm probably in the wrong for straying into his path. I argue he rammed me. He didn't see me because it was raining hard and he was going at a good clip on a very stormy night with practically no visibility. They don't really seem to care.

The tug captain has wandered off to his boat. With my duffel bag I wander off too, into the town of Dover to an old motel and fourteen hours of uninterrupted sleep. The next day, feeling very much alone in the world, I'm off to Philadelphia.

The bus rumbles past farms, bridges and rivers but I hardly notice. Deep in thought I wonder if the sloop was meant to take the place of my father. The old man doled out discipline and so did the *Martha Jane*. It made you work. On land there was priming and painting, mending and cleaning, on rough water you never let up. They both pushed me. There was something else. The *Martha Jane* was my last connection to Parrsboro. Now it's torn and twisted beneath the waters of Delaware Bay. Once again my direction is gone.

Philadelphia looms up at me, the skyline swelling above the dirty windows of the bus. It takes a long time through city streets to reach the main terminal. I find a hotel and spend time looking through the phone book, writing down numbers. The Pennsylvania athletic commission gives me another number to call; at city hall, they give me another number. By five o'clock I have the address of a recommended boxing promoter in good standing with the commission and city authorities. I am taking no chances, with enough money for a month and no sloop to live on, hotels will gobble up my cash. I need to fight fast and I have a name. The authoritative voice on the phone tells me, "We really can't recommend anyone but let me say George Bryson is a man with a very good reputation."

His office is off Vine Street in the heart of Philadelphia. The next morning I set out to find him. I'm both hopeful and weary. My optimism builds a little when I enter his office. It has the look of respectability: a secretary, filing cabinets, photographs of fighters on the wall. Different from the booze, cards, smoke and bluster of Victor's.

Bryson can't see me right away. His secretary says it could be awhile. What have I got to do? I wait almost an hour.

George Bryson apologizes with a friendly grin and a solid handshake. He's a middle-aged man with reddish brown hair and friendly eyes. He sits me down in a big leather chair and asks me questions.

It's as if I'm being interviewed for a job. He's the first person I've had to talk to since the sinking and it all comes pouring out of me. I try to hold back but I can't. I'm a verbal waterfall, spewing information on everything — boxing, Parrsboro, the *Martha Jane*, sailing and sinking. I don't touch Boston or Victor or any of that. When I tell him about the sinking his mouth opens in disbelief. When I finish he shakes his head and says, "Unbelievable."

"It is," I answer.

Things are different in Philadelphia. Here they play by the rules and there are a lot of rules when it comes to boxing. I need an out-of-state license, a medical certificate, and this and that. My head is spinning as he talks.

"Will you represent me?" I ask.

He smiles, "That depends on how well you can fight."

There's no sense holding back. I let him in on my financial situation: I'm nearly broke.

He shakes his head sadly.

"I couldn't put you on a fight card for six weeks at least and I'm not promising you anything, except I'll look at you. I represent sixteen fighters and all of them have a shot at a title. I don't carry dead-weight. You need money and a place to stay," he says and picks up the phone.

Bryson has connections. He moves me to another hotel near his gym and gets me a temporary job at a warehouse near Chinatown. I will spar for him Saturday.

The job is only for a couple of weeks. It's heavy lifting, work that will get me back in shape, and by five o'clock the following day my arms and back feel the strain. My work mates are Portuguese or Italian, big guys who talk about sex and beer. After work I join them at a nearby bar. They poke fun at me because I'm drinking Coke. They are gruff and rough men, but they like boxing and despite the teasing they're friendly.

My hotel is old and cheap, full of prostitutes and intoxicated men, people bumming money and offering things for sale. The man behind the counter has a scar on his face and looks mean and bored. At night in my room I put on my gloves and shadowbox, getting back to the bob and weave.

I call my mother, but don't tell her about the *Martha Jane*. She's surprised I'm in Philadelphia but delighted to hear from me.

"I thought you were in Boston."

"There weren't any opportunities there. Are you all right?"

"I'm fine. Are you all right? I'm so glad to hear from you, I've been so worried."

"I'll be in Philadelphia for several weeks. I've got a fight here with a big time promoter. How's Heather?" I ask.

"She calls in on me every couple of weeks asking about you. She's going into nursing."

"She's always wanted that. Tell her I said hi."

"She always talks about you, and the Hunters and everybody want to know how you're doing. Duff, I worry. I had this awful dream. Your boat . . . never mind, it was just a nightmare."

She says she misses the old man. He was a challenge, from tirade to tenderness in ten seconds, complaining one minute, telling jokes the next.

"It's so lonely without him and with you gone."

I have left her alone. Mr. Big Adventure is now lifting boxes in Philadelphia.

I walk out of the crummy hotel, past stores and vacant buildings, restaurants and offices. It feels good to be in the night air, as if I were standing on the deck of the *Martha Jane*.

Saturday I arrive at the gym thirty minutes early. Bryson introduces me to his trainer, who sends me into a changing room. My sparring partner is a veteran boxer named Earl Tugboat Targatt. In front of me, Bryson tells Earl to show me no mercy. He wants to see what I've got.

"This is baptism by fire, Duff. You make it or break it right here."

I make it. Earl is sent to the mat early with a left hook.

There are murmurs around the ring and Bryson says, "Good punch or lucky punch, Duff. What was it?" I smile and try to promote some cockiness I don't feel.

"Usual punch," I reply.

He puts me with another fighter named Juan. Young, slender with liquid muscles, Juan is better than Earl, very fast and a very good counterpuncher. We're going at it. I fire hard jabs, trying to make them count. Move my feet as he throws a right and I hit him with a left hook and a jab. He comes back, wiry and strong and incredibly fast.

The old man would be cursing me now because I'm not concentrating but seeing things around me, like the dozen men hanging over the ropes watching us. The only sound in the gym is us, our punches. I pay for letting my mind wander: he gets me with a solid right that sends me reeling backward. I hear the old man's words, "Bear down!"

I know what to do, keep him away while I regain my concentration. I ram the hurt to the back of my brain. I keep my gloves high and my feet move faster, dancing away, jab in quickly then away, the old bob and weave, practiced on Shorty and Snooky but mostly on the old man, practiced on people in the classroom and friends in the hallway, on guys on the street and the family dog. I'm the master of the bob and weave. He's trying to catch me and as he advances I come at him with a right hook that misses but a left that hits him. My feet are moving and I let the right go again. It gets him hard on the forehead. Now he's dancing and bobbing and weaving, now he's got his feet in high gear, staying away from me.

"Enough," cries Bryson. Juan and I touch gloves. Like the tug skipper who sank me I can't understand a word he says. Bryson sends me to the showers and then buys me lunch.

"I'll put you on my fight card for the sixteenth of next month, provided you train every day. If you win, I'll take you on as one of my fighters. If you lose you get three hundred dollars and a good bye. You understand?" I do.

"You're fighting Juan and I think you should know the money will be on him. Juan is considered an up and coming middleweight. I saw him fight in the Dominican Republic last year and brought him stateside. He's never faced a fighter like you. That was obvious today," he laughs.

"What do you mean, like me?"

"You're tall. Juan will have to punch up at you, meaning a big change in his stance, but it's something he'll have to do if he goes up through the ranks. Also you're a hard hitter, you have a better punch than most middleweights. A credit to your training," he says.

"A credit to my father," I say.

110

"Beat him and you'll be on your way, but I think you know he's very good."

He doesn't have to tell me. My face stings.

"This will be Juan's second fight in the States, a Dominican against a Canadian. Train hard. I want a good fight and may the best man win."

"He will," I say. There's that old cockiness again.

2 3

FIGHTING IN PHILADELPHIA

My routine is torture — up at five-thirty, at the warehouse by seven, nights at the gym, working the big bag, skipping and sparring with another middleweight named Javier.

He's Mexican, been boxing ten years and has the face to show it: a broken nose, misshapen ears, missing teeth, but he's full of good humor. He tells me stories of growing up in Mexico, of poverty and hard times, of getting to the States, which he always calls the USA. Once rated number four in the world, he's had some big fights and made some major money, married his childhood sweetheart, has six children. Javier is very proud of his house, that's bought and paid for. He is careful with his defensive position and with his money. At twenty-eight he is on his way down but doesn't acknowledge it. Boxing is a fast train, from top to bottom. The saddest thing is not knowing when to get off.

Javier is saving all the money he can. Even so, he lends me twenty bucks. I need money for food. I can't skip lunch or dinner on this routine. Some days I try to exist on a fifty-cent breakfast at Hays Bickford, lunch at the diner with guys from the warehouse, beans and toast and milk. I have a sandwich before the gym and as big a meal as I can afford afterward.

When Javier picks me up at my hotel for a Sunday dinner at his place, he feels so sorry for me he suggests I move in with his family until after the fight.

"Man, you can't live here!"

The offer touches me but he's already got a full house.

His children are polite and polished. His wife Carmelita is a big woman with a pretty face, who tells me she hopes she has not put so much spice and peppers in the main course in case I'm not used to hot food. Despite their good manners the children can't contain themselves when tears run down my face. They laugh openly as I gulp a gallon of water. This is a happy household except when Javier mentions the fight; then I sense a certain tension. This family has a lot riding on what Javier calls his come-back fight. He faces a young Rhodesian by the name of Augustus Motellie who has a left jab, they say, that sounds like the crack of a bull whip. Javier is my only friend in Philadelphia. I'm hoping for the best for both of us.

Fight night will be at the Philadelphia Sports Arena on Patterson Avenue. The headliners are heavyweights Chester Mathas and Bobby Knox. It amazes me I'm higher on the card than Javier. They are playing up the nationalities of Juan and myself but don't mention it in Javier's fight. There is no Mexican verses Rhodesian.

In the last few days now, they check my weight and I ease up on training. Bryson takes me out of the warehouse. I spar only twice a day but he gives me a number of good sparring partners.

Juan is watching me. He studies my stride, my footwork, looking for a weakness. I do the same to him, always impressed with his speed. His quick hands have bullet speed. People around the gym stop and watch when he spars.

The sixteenth is here. I sleep in and splurge on lunch, treat myself to steak and potatoes and greens. I eat with Javier in a restaurant in downtown Philadelphia off Broad Street. We don't talk much, getting mentally ready, alone inside ourselves.

All Bryson's fighters meet at the gym three hours before fight time. He talks to us in a group. Bryson is a quiet man and he gives us a gentle talk, about boxing and being mentally ready to handle pain and to have courage. It's a far cry from the old man's bluster and not what I expect from a big city boxing manager. There is another medical and more forms to sign, a final weigh-in and then cars take us to the arena. The event is very organized. We are assigned changing rooms followed by visits by representatives of the Pennsylvania Athletic Authority. Then trainers tape our hands.

Juan is in the next room. I wonder what's going through his mind. I wonder what's going through mine. I'm not nervous and it bothers me how disconnected and detached I feel.

Javier comes in and hugs me, and goes off to meet his destiny. I wait alone now and somehow think of my first big fight in Moncton. Wish Dewey was here or even Lawrence. I wish Danny was here, even if he was getting sick on himself.

I smile despite myself. A member of the Parrsboro Boxing Club fighting tonight in Philadelphia. If Juan hits me I don't think I'll feel it. I'm above pain right now, above human emotion — just somehow empty. I usually hate that time just before a fight, full of nervous energy made worse by the crowd noise. I hear the crowd but it doesn't excite me. Why?

They bring Javier back on a stretcher, the doctor holding a cloth to his head. He was knocked out in the third round. The Rhodesian's rapid left hand, once, twice, three times to Javier's head. There is swelling around the eye. He is coming to, twitching, his leg moving, his face wet and swollen. I only see him because I'm outside my dressing room now, robe on, ready to go.

I can't stay, it's my turn. Two men I have never seen before walk with me down the aisle to the ring. It's a long walk in a humid and noisy building. Funny, I thought the old man would be in my head tonight, but I have to work to think of him at all. He's washed his hands of me. He hasn't been with me since I glided out of Boston in the middle of the night.

Juan is in the ring when I get there. He's got gold trunks with a black stripe. He's trying to look like a winner, dancing, moving his gloves above his head, gesturing to an army of boisterous supporters sitting directly behind him — his family of brothers, sisters, aunts, uncles, his mother, his old man and a gray-haired stooped woman. He's brought his aging parents from the Dominican Republic to support him. I'm trying to feel something, to work up some hostility. I look at the frail couple in the center of his cheering section. The prick, forcing his old parents all the way here. Bastard. Behind Juan even the seniors try to cheer, toothless old uncles in black suits, young cousins in white shirts, nieces in print dresses. Four young men, probably brothers, are in the front row. They keep jumping up and down, screaming in Spanish. A sizable, noisy section and he reacts to them.

Behind me are sullen expressions and no friendly faces. Is that why I feel so dried up? I remember boxing in the church yard at Fox River, near Parrsboro. It was a hot Sunday afternoon. I literally tingled inside with nervous energy. It made me ready to explode. I need that feeling now.

Flashbulbs popping, cheers and catcalls, thousands of people and not one of them knows me except Bryson and that dazed Mexican down in the dressing room. Javier's family waits at home. Do they already know?

Juan doesn't look at me during the ref's instructions, won't make eye contact. I try to put on my dirty face, my killer mask, but I don't know if it really looks mean. The bell is ringing and the fight I've traveled to and waited for is underway.

Juan gets aggressive right away. He tries a series of jabs to my head and gets his family in a frenzy right from the start. I hit him with a good body blow; he gets off a combination that tags me. We dance, strike, reposition and dance again. He punches, I punch; he waits, I wait. We are both fast and hard hitters and there is an audible sound to our blows, the "waps" and "smacks" and "swooshes" and "slaps." The crowd responds to every punch. He is trying to get inside, wants body blows. He persists and I keep dancing. Then I go for him with a fake left and hit him with a right; he counters and the first round ends.

The next three rounds are much the same — defensive, careful, we're not taking chances. He's waiting for me. I'm waiting for him. Some of his jabs are getting to me. I change my stance, but he's getting at me more than I want.

In round five things change. I put him into the ropes with a solid right hook, my best punch of the fight. His family is jumping up and down, shouting in Spanish as I take advantage of my punch. I throw another hook that misses; he counters with a right hand that gets me in the face, hard like steel — I wince. He's throwing very fast jabs to my cheek, like pinpricks. Then a piece of steel, hard below my left eye. Real pain, then pinpricks again.

Finally in the sixth I hear the old man's voice, not his excitable voice. It's soft, most unlike him.

"Get on your horse and dance, use those legs, move, dance."

"Where've you been?" I silently scream. "Where, when I'm needing you?"

There is no answer. For Christ sake! Who am I fighting — Juan or the old man? Why am I so upset? What father ever spent more time with his son? What father ever devoted more of his life to his son's boxing? The hours and hours spent together, why am I so angry? Just as the bell ends round six I know. A son wants other things. Going fishing, to movies or other things. We did only one thing, over and over again — boxing, boxing, boxing, month after month, year after year. I know at this moment what's been eating away at me since his death. I wanted more of him. I wanted other things. What a confusing night. I'm learning things about myself as I box in front of thousands of people. I'm losing this fight but I suddenly feel relief. The tension is draining out of me.

The trainer and doctor are over me. "I'm fine," I plead. They look skeptical but the fight continues. Before the bell rings for the seventh round Juan is on his feet, accepting cheers from his family. He looks cocky.

My legs are rubbery as I keep away from his jabs. I'm trying for a big right. It misses and he counters into my midsection, hard. I feel the breath leaving my body in a gust. Suddenly starved for oxygen I suck in hot sweaty air. There is steel in my face again like I've been hit with a half inch pipe. Then I don't recognize this. What is it? What happened? It's so, so black.

The lights have gone out and my guts are on fire. I'm bending and can't stop. There is no order to my body, no command I can give. I'm on the *Martha Jane* in that hellish sea off Maine. The deck is moving, I'm losing my footing. I'm what? Falling, I am falling, and hitting the canvas, dirty canvas, spit, groan, hard fall, old man, wait, he's here, I can hear him, "GET UP!" No, it's not him, it's them. "Get up," they're yelling at me, all of them, the old man, Curly, Snooky, Jack Ryan, Lawrence, Dewey.

People are over me, people I don't know. I'm on my feet now and Juan is taking bows and being very cocky. Never be cocky, kid. Didn't your old man tell you that? What the hell's wrong with you?

Stay there, mister, whoever you are. Let me lean on you. You're my cane, when I move you move. Arms around me. Juan is putting his arms around me and hugs me. Puts his gloves on my shoulders and says something. I nod but haven't got a clue. What's the difference. I'm moving out of the ring now, down the aisle toward the dressing rooms, the helpful stranger keeps me up. It's Bryson holding me; he is my cane.

They are kind folks in Philadelphia, kind comments, more than I deserve. "Good fight, kid," they yell. Kind folks but liars all of them. It was an awful fight. I could be angry, could be upset, but I'm too dizzy right now. I lost, came all this way, lost the fight, lost the sloop, lost, well, maybe not everything. Maybe tonight in the middle of a fight I found something too.

In the dressing room the doctor looks me over. He wants an X-ray and that means they will take me to the hospital soon. All I want is a shower. A long, hard, hot shower to wash off the defeat. The water runs and runs. Slowly it comes to me how god-awful it is to lose.

When I come back from the shower, Bryson is standing in my dressing room. He smiles at me. "You did fine, Duff," handing me a cheque and a hundred dollars in cash for a total of three hundred.

"Give me another chance. I can do better."

As Juan did earlier, he puts his hand on my shoulder.

"Duff, your boxing ability is good. You could hang around this division for a few years, maybe win a few big fights." He looks me straight in the eyes. "But in my humble opinion from what I've seen, you're not going to be," he shakes his head, "a champion." He then takes a heavy breath. "Hear it from me. You're good, you're fast, you're strong. But I can only carry fighters with a chance of going all the way to the top. You're good, but you're not good enough." He squeezes my shoulder.

"I can only be honest with you, Duff. You could go up against Juan again but he'd beat you again. And there are young fighters out there now in the middleweight division who can beat him. Juan may make it, if he works hard, if he's lucky, but even for him it will be an uphill struggle and he's got talent, more natural talent than you." He smiles, trying to soften the words. "It's not your fault. It's just the way it is." He pats my shoulder and turns toward the door. After a couple of steps he faces me again. "Another thing. He wants it more, a lot more."

He's gone — got other priorities, other fighters.

I lean against the wall and slowly sink to the floor and stay very still. Bryson's words ring in my ears, cutting something deep into me: "Good, but not good enough" and "He wants it more." So different from the old man's words. "You can be a champ," he'd say. Yet this is it, isn't it. Bryson is right. He's telling me the truth and the old man could never distinguish between what he wanted and what was possible. He couldn't drag that bum leg through the division so he tried to drag me, and I let him, because he was my old man and I loved him.

Maybe tonight I've finally found myself. A hell of a long way from the Parrsboro Boxing Club but at this moment I know I'm going back to Parrsboro and more importantly I know why. I dress slowly, pack my duffel bag and put on my jacket. I'm skipping the X-ray.

It's only then that I think of Javier. I find him in a dressing room down the hall. He's alone, still in his boxing shorts, sitting on the rubdown table. Bryson has cut him loose as well. His career is over. If there ever was a sad sight, this is it. Broken-nosed, cauliflower-eared, gap-toothed Javier. Javier the happy one, bawling his eyes out. I would comfort him but there is no comfort to give.

"You'll get another shot." Such feeble words, such lies, would be better left unsaid. He looks at me. "I have nothing but my house, not enough to put my children in good schools, not enough to give them something, something lasting."

"You have a very nice house, that's something."

"It's a roof and walls," he sobs. "It's not enough. All my life I dream of more, promise my children good schools. What am I going to do? My children will never have their dreams, dreams I promised them." He cries some more as I stand there looking at him. "I needed this fight. I needed another shot at the title." He looks so pathetic but I have no words. I put my arms around him the way my old man did to me when there were no words, when we'd used up the language. We embrace for a long minute. I turn and walk out of the room, down the corridor into the night. There is nothing more I can do for him.

I hail a cab to my hotel, pay the bill, get a bus schedule and I'm off again into the dark streets of Philadelphia. The bus terminal is twenty blocks but I walk. I'll be sitting long enough, to Trenton, New Jersey, then Newark, then Bangor, Maine, then Saint John, New Brunswick, then home. Going home with a sense that something is over. What I'm going to do next I'm going to do for myself. I'm going to build another sloop and I'm going to call it the *Heather* and I'm going to lose a friend in Danny.

It starts to rain, just a light mist cooling my face. The streets are almost deserted. I walk alone, feeling Manny's spy glass in my duffel bag with every step I take. The Jack Johnson photograph is under my arm. For the first time tonight I feel energized, as if something heavy is gone, lifted off me. At one corner of the bus terminal there is a large garbage can. I swing the duffel bag off my shoulder, take out my boxing gloves and drop them in, one at a time. It's over. No more training, no more steel in my face, no more Victors. I don't want to be ten years older and be left like Javier. The old man's dream is done. I have to find my own dream. I will. I stand there a long moment looking at the gloves and then I drop the Johnson photograph in as well. The lights of the terminal reflect on the glass, showing the big black man on his back, his career finished.

"Good bye."

Near the terminal door two boys are entertaining themselves. Maybe twelve or thirteen, they are out late and hamming it up. Their reflections in the terminal's lights cast long shadows on the pavement in front of the building. The taller one is dancing, moving his head and using his feet with his fists in front of him. He's showing his stuff to the smaller boy who is also ducking and shuffling. I recognize it immediately. It's the old hive and jive, the old move and groove, the old bob and weave.

119

24

GOING HOME

The end of the second day on the bus we're deep in the woods of Maine. It's dark and the road is rough. I take Manny's spy glass out of my duffel bag and fall asleep with it in my hands. We stop at a little diner and I get some coffee and settle down for the next few hours to Bangor. The bus is half full of dozing passengers, movement and muffled sounds: murmured conversations, an occasional click of a cigarette lighter, the crackle of a turning newspaper page, the soft hum of the motor — a good place to think.

What am I going to tell people? Like all small towns, Parrsboro has big ears. In a city you can hide things; in a small town you live in the open, barefaced before your neighbors. There is little point in trying to pretend. I lost the boat and the fight and boxing is behind me. How do I explain that to people who believed I could be a champion?

Bangor has plenty of spirals and steeples, brick buildings and white houses. During the two-hour stop in the early morning I walk around the empty downtown. Bookstores, secondhand shops, restaurants and a furniture store. I look in the windows of all of them. There is nothing I need or want. On one side street there is a boarded-up door with a tattered boxing poster. It's for a fight long since fought. Kid Stewart and Shane O'Day, ten rounds. The paper is ripped and soggy. Only the ends of its torn pieces are dry enough to move back and forth in the light breeze. Two young fighters in their stance, gloves in front of them. They're ready to take on the world. Kid Stewart's face is missing but the picture of O'Day is intact. Serious, he's showing his best stuff. I spend a long time standing on the sidewalk staring at him, wondering what happened. Where is he now? Did he feel that steel in his head? Was his old man with him?

A depression settles over me as I walk back to the bus. I've let a lot of people down. My mother, however, will be happy. I haven't called her since Philadelphia. Maybe tonight I'll call. And Heather will be glad I'm through with boxing and, I hope, happy to see me.

As the bus lumbers through the back streets of Bangor we see children with brightly colored hoops. They're putting them around their waists and rotating their hips, keeping the hoops in motion. They're girls maybe seven or eight years old and they can't keep the things going very long.

"Them's hula hoops," says the wrinkled lady across the aisle. "Bought one for my granddaughter."

"I've never seen them before," I reply.

"You can blame it all on that Elvis Presley, him moving his hips and all, got all the young people doing it now. It's indecent but what you going to do, they want, want, want and hound you till you gives in."

She squirms in her seat and tells me her church group has officially condemned Elvis. The secretary wrote a letter to the Bishop. She looks out the window and draws on a long cigarette.

"My granddaughter got trouble with her school work, but knows all the words to "Hound Dog" and "Blue Suede Shoes." Elvis is the devil himself." Then she moves her big sad face towards me, smiles and says, "Boy can sing if he'd just keep his hips still. It's indecent. I kinda like Pat Boone myself."

We're back in the woods. No more hula-hooping children or white picket fences. Now it's pine, spruce and low rolling hills. The old lady and I talk about the Russians, who she says are an even bigger threat than Elvis. "At least he's not up there zooming around in space." She laughs. Her favorite movie is *High Noon* with Gary

Cooper. "Typical — your friends turn their back on you when you need their help." She draws on her cigarette and I fall asleep.

We're given forms at the Canada-U.S. border and the customs man is giving me a hard time.

"How come you've been in the States for three months with no visa or work permit? Please explain that to me."

"I went down there to box. I sailed down."

"But you didn't declare yourself. Officially you never entered the United States."

"If that's the case, where have I been?"

"You've been in the United States illegally, that's where you've been."

"Why do you care? You're Canadian."

Tired and irritable I'm going toe to toe with this jerk. He gets his supervisor, who takes me into an office and shuts the door.

"Where's your boat?"

When I tell him he doesn't believe me.

"You sold the boat and pocketed the cash, didn't you?"

"The U.S. Coast Guard has a record of the sinking."

"We'll check. Until we do you're staying here."

The bus leaves without me. The little old lady is the last face I see as it pulls away. I'm in a small room with white walls, two chairs, a table and a lamp. Old magazines and old furniture. I want to close my fist and slam it into something.

In a copy of *Life* magazine there is the feature on the Russian Sputnik. The Russians are in space whirling around the earth and I'm stuck in a customs house in Houlton, Maine. Maybe the customs people will throw me in jail and it will be a long time before I get home.

I stretch out on a vinyl chair with a small rip running along the seat and stuffing sticking out. I close my eyes and take a few deep breaths.

I'm in the ring with Snooky Redden. His boxing gloves are made out of the same fawn-colored vinyl in the chair. One glove is ripped and the stuffing is coming out.

"New gloves, Duff, your old man isn't here to save you this time. New gloves, Duff, gloves to beat you with."

He hauls back and spits and a volley of water flies over my shoulder as he presses a furious attack, both vinyl gloves flying. He dances back and forth. There is blood on his gloves.

"Snooky, you don't understand. I'm through, no more fighting, I'm not boxing anymore."

He grins, a horrible rotting-tooth grin, and sneers, "Coward."

2 5

Home

Back on a bus my hours are filled with similar dreams. All the buildings in Parrsboro are painted yellow — stores on Main Street, the bandstand, the churches, the schools all yellow. Dewey is standing next to the hardware store. His clothes are yellow and he's got a paintbrush in his hand.

"Welcome home, Duff, we did it all for you."

I awake with a chill. Leaving was easier than coming home.

We roll into Parrsboro at 10:45 in the evening. The streets are bleak and bare and the town looks smaller — shrunken in three months. I didn't call my mother so there is no one to meet me.

With my duffel bag I walk home down Main Street. Wheaton's restaurant is open but I don't even look in, just keep walking to our house in Whitehall.

The dreams have left a chill and now an even more uncomfortable thought comes over me. What if my mother has company, male company? What if I interrupt something important? I feel the guilt all children feel when they think sexual things about their parents.

The porch light is on and our '52 Studebaker is in the driveway. I stop at the door. Do I knock, walk in or ring the bell? I ring the bell once and walk in. "Hello," I repeat through the kitchen. The television is on and I hear footsteps. She is in the doorway to the living room. Surprised, a small pleased yelp comes out of her. Like the town, she also looks smaller and more fragile.

"Duff! Oh, my God!" She flies into my arms. "I've been so worried!"

It is a night of conversation and coffee. We sit in the living room and I tell her everything. The whale, Manny, Boston, Baltimore Bay, the *Martha Jane* sinking and Philadelphia. She cries and laughs and hugs me and serves more coffee. She brings out some tea cakes and we eat them all. She fills me in on Parrsboro. How Curly is having a hard time keeping the club together. How Dewey is doing in college, how Lawrence has been bringing her lobster and flounder. She tells me about the school and the church.

"How's Heather?" I ask and there is a small smile, the look she used to give me when I filled the woodbox without being asked or brought home a well-colored picture from school.

"She and Danny broke up about a month ago. She's started nursing training in Halifax."

"Is she seeing anybody?"

"I don't know. She comes home some weekends and always asks about you. I haven't had much to tell her. Duff, why didn't you tell me about losing the sloop?"

"I didn't want you to worry. Actually, I didn't think much about losing the *Martha Jane*. I put it out of my mind."

I don't tell her about my strange dreams on the bus. When I go upstairs my bedroom also looks smaller. There is a photograph on my wall of the old man and me taken after my first big victory in Moncton. He has his arm around me and he's wearing the world's biggest smile. It's taken by the same camera that took the Joe Louis pictures in New York. The old man gave it to Curly and put his arm around me.

"Proud of you, kid." I stand there a long time looking at it.

The next day I start making up for the months I've been gone. There is a lot to do: painting a ceiling, splitting wood, dragging the fridge out and cleaning behind it, taking down the living room curtains. By late afternoon I'm ready for some air and I go for the mail. Sitting on the post office steps is Mouse. He is almost as happy to see me as my mother was.

"God Almighty, am I glad to see you! God, you're a sight for sore eyes." It takes him a few minutes to finally ask, "What are you doing here anyway? How come you're home?"

Here's my test — the first explanation why I'm home. Despite practice on the bus I can't quite do it.

"I missed you, Mouse."

His big bear paws are around me.

"Missed you, buddy."

Oh well. We walk up the street for a coffee.

"I'm giving Curly a hand in the club. Frankie Henwood is doing real good, won another bout in Amherst and may go to Halifax for a fight in January. When are you going to fight?"

On this question I can't avoid the truth.

"I'm not, Mouse. I went to Philadelphia and fought the fastest man I've ever seen. He beat me fair and square and I'm not going back in the ring."

He just looks at me.

"How come?" he finally booms as other customers and waitresses look at us.

"Because I'm through with boxing."

"But you're the best there is, Duff. You can't quit."

"I already have, Mouse."

He's quiet for awhile and sips his coffee.

"Heather is going to be a nurse. You know she and asshole broke up."

"Still mad at Danny?" I ask and immediately regret the question.

"I'd like to kill the little fucker. He wants her back, ya know, tries everything. I tell her Danny is an asshole. She still carries a big suitcase for you, buddy. I hope you cram that little prick right out of the field."

Mouse has been angry at Danny since the incident with the hooker. He feels Danny caused him a lot of his troubles by blabbing all over town that he was arrested and taken to jail and is now a man with a record. Dewey says it's all part of the strange world of Mouse, since it was Mouse himself who told everybody. Danny and Mouse had words over it and Danny demanded an apology and told Mouse off. Mouse's response was to take a swing at Danny right in front of Dot Taylor's hat shop.

"Mouse, you almost took out the window in the millinery store," Dewey told him.

"God, Dew, what are you talking about? It was the hat shop and I wasn't that close to the window."

Mouse tells me he has hardly seen Danny lately. Which, under the circumstances, may be just as well.

We're having coffee in Wheaton's, listening to the jukebox. Burke's has the best pinball machine, Wheaton's the best jukebox. They've spruced up the interior. Green vinyl booths and green uniforms for the waitresses and big colored photographs on the walls. Local landmarks, rocky shores, beaches and driftwood. It's not busy; two waitresses sit in the back booth smoking. Somebody puts a nickel in the jukebox. Patti Page is singing "The Tennessee Waltz," "I was dancing with my sweetheart — "

It's like I never left, like it was all a dream. Then Mouse snaps me back to reality.

"I'm going back to boxin'. What d'ya think? Would ya help me train? I mean, ya know, would you help me?"

"No, Mouse, I won't."

26

CURLY

Heather hears two things: I'm home and I've changed. When she gets home from Halifax Friday night, Mouse is waiting on her back steps. She leaves Mouse having tea with her mother and walks to my place. There isn't any talk — we're in each other's arms in seconds. I'm kissing her the way I've wanted to for months.

"I want to know one thing," she says. "I can't go on like this — it's killing me. Breaking up, missing you, worrying about you — tell me, I have to know, do you love me?"

I kiss her again. The agony of missing her is seeping out of me.

We make love this night under the cold November sky, laying our coats side by side in a small field surrounded by spruce trees. We don't feel the chill.

"I'm never letting you go."

"Please keep that promise."

Happiness sweeps over me but two days later Curly shows up, bringing my past with him. I've been expecting him and dreading it.

"Duff," he says over tea in our kitchen, "the club needs you. We need you to help us keep things going."

"I can't, Curly. I've got to put boxing behind me and get on with my life."

"Boxing is your life."

Curly's quickness can catch you. He stutters sometimes and doesn't seem sharp and then he throws you a retort like a high level debater.

"Not anymore, it isn't."

"Duff, your father put so much into boxing, into your training. Don't throw that away."

How much do I want to explain? I know he's desperate. The time he's put in the club and the help he's been to the old man — I owe him an explanation.

It's difficult because Curly isn't buying a bit of it. We talk for an hour. I tell him about Philadelphia and my fight against Juan. When I finish he doesn't say anything, just looks at me. He is cross-eyed and it's hard to tell exactly where he's looking. He moves a hand through his comb-over and then puts his hands together on the table.

"Got anything stronger than tea?"

The old man kept a bottle of rum in the basement. Curly takes a big drink and starts to talk. He opens up to me.

"You know I live with my sister, never had any other family. Came back from the war and worked at the liquor store and didn't do nothing except follow baseball and boxing. My sister hates sports, hates drinking, hates almost everything."

He tells me intimate details of his life and the only love affair he's ever had.

"Except for the war and those girls in France — I spent as much time as I could with them, more than most guys. Almost as if I could look ahead and know there wasn't going to be a woman for me. When Maggie picked me up two years ago and drove me home from a ball game one night, I got up all my nerve, more than I thought I had, and asked her if she wanted a cup of coffee and some fries. We drove over to the pier and parked and I felt her up. Next night I walked out to her house. That's over four miles from my place but I walked. I don't have a car and I couldn't make up my mind whether to walk through town right up Main Street or take the back streets, but I thought I'd be more, what's the word?"

"Obvious?"

"Yes, obvious. I thought it would look more obvious if I was walking down them back streets. Nosy people lookin' out their windows, saying where the hell's Curly goin'? So I walked right up Main Street, every time I went to see her."

He's talking about Maggie Innis. No secret Maggie likes men and doesn't take her marriage vows too seriously but her and Curly! Balding, cross-eyed Curly is pouring his third drink at my kitchen table, telling his life's story. I grab a glass and join him.

"I called her last winter," he says. "Told her I was comin' out that night. Then it started to snow and the wind came up. Howling and blowing like hell. I walked to her house, anyway, four miles through the snow. Walked right up the middle of Main Street and Eastern Avenue — nobody driving, no plows. The wind howled and the power went out. You walk half a mile out there between houses, but I kept going. Didn't get there till eleven o'clock and pounded on her door. My hands were so cold I couldn't feel them beating on her door. She was surprised as hell to see me. I was covered in snow and wet right through."

Curly's hand is shaking and he takes another drink.

"Maggie sat me by her wood stove and took my clothes off. She rubbed me down with a big towel and put me under her covers. I spent the night there, Duff, didn't get home till the next afternoon. It was the only time I stayed away all night. Imagine. I'm fifty-two years old and Maggie was my first piece of tail since the war. I don't have much, Duff, not much at all. My sister kept nagging, wanted to know where I was all night. She thought I'd died. Finally I get fed up and tell her I was with a woman. 'Committing immorality!' she screams and shuts up. Which is fine with me, I like the quiet."

He looks at me over the top of his glasses.

"I know Maggie is a bit of a whore but she's always been good to me. Her husband came home this spring and that ended that."

He looks out the window over our front lawn. "I should have got married a long time ago."

His glasses are sliding down his nose and there is desperation in his voice.

"Duff, I love that club and it's slipping away. Guys won't train, don't come to sparring sessions. Help me, Duff, please."

I put my head in my hands. He was the old man's best friend and supporter and he's touched me.

"Curly, I want to get away from boxing."

"Help me until the spring. Just until Frankie Henwood is ready for a shot at a pro career. He's big and strong and good enough."

I look at him.

"Please, Duff."

"All right, Curly."

27

MOUSE ON THE TABLE

A small town newspaper boils down your life to bare essentials, like sap being reduced to make maple sugar. Gallons and gallons boiled down to a tiny sugary syrup. *The Parrsboro Record* runs a small story about Mr. Duff Martin "returning from a visit to the United States where, due to an unfortunate accident near Philadelphia, his sloop the *Martha Jane* was lost. Friends will be happy to hear Duff was not injured. Duff is a well-known boxer and son of Mrs. Jean Martin and the late Alex Martin of Parrsboro."

A visit to the United States!

After a week people are used to seeing me around and questions slow down. I get a job working with Rob Davieson, a local electrician, and Dewey's father promises me some work on his fishing boats. It is quiet in Parrsboro; most of my friends are gone and Heather only comes home two weekends a month.

Tuesday nights, usually gritting my teeth, I go to the boxing club and work with Frankie Henwood. I expect the old man's hand on my shoulder at any minute so I have to concentrate hard on Frankie. He is a good boxer, a very strong light heavyweight.

"Spar with me, Duff, for old time's sake," Frankie pleads. I laugh it off.

"I'm a middleweight, Frankie, you want to kill me?"

Mouse joins the army but comes back to the club until he gets his call for basic training. The night before he leaves we have dinner at Burke's.

"Duff, I'm going to box in the army. Think I can?"

"Keep some kind of defense going and yes, you've got the offense. But Curly or I aren't going to be there to keep reminding you, it's something you have to do yourself."

He thinks about this and suddenly says, "If I stay in twenty years I get a pension and can retire here and help you and Curly run the club."

"Twenty years is a long time, Mouse. Who says we'll be here in twenty years?"

"Well, if you are."

Mouse has been seeing Lucy Armstrong and I wonder why he isn't spending his last night with her.

"OK, Mouse, what's with you and Lucy?" His big head drops as if it's going to fall into his food.

"Problems," he says and stirs his fork around his hot chicken sandwich.

"Oh," I say and leave it at that. After we eat and play the pinball machine, we walk down to Canning's taxi stand where there is one pool table and we start playing eight ball. It's snowing outside and the place is empty.

During the second game Mouse starts talking about Lucy. She invited him for lunch when her parents went shopping in Amherst. Their car broke down in Southampton.

"Lucy made us burgers and fries and, ya know, I was feeling kind of frisky and started, ya know, fooling around, tickling her and grabbing her ass and we started hugging and kissing."

I'm already sorry I mentioned Lucy and try to change subjects but now Mouse wants to talk, to tell me everything. God, I just listened to Curly's confidential three weeks ago and don't want to hear another one. Mouse, however, is in full flight.

"Then we ate the burgers and we started again and first thing I knew my hand is under her sweater feeling her tits and we're kissing and then she started, ya know, stroking me."

He's getting excited and missing shots. Sex and pool don't mix.

"We're naked on the table."

"On the table?"

"Yeah, on the table, on the kitchen table."

"What did you do with the dishes and things?"

"Moved most of them. Forks and stuff just kinda fell on the floor."

"God, Mouse, why the kitchen table?"

"I don't know, it was the closest place."

He stands close to me.

"Shit, it was awful. We're bare-assed on the table and in walk her parents and her little brother. Her mother shrieks, her brother points and laughs and her old man dances around, yelling. Lucy starts bawling. God, the noise was awful. Allison, that little shit brother of hers, is jumping up and down screaming, 'You got caught fucking! You got caught fucking!' The old man gives him a swat and he starts bawling and the old guy comes at me. I'm hopping around the kitchen trying to put on my pants."

I try not to laugh. It's the image of big Mouse hopping around half naked, chased by little Archie Armstrong.

Mouse isn't laughing.

"He pinned me against the wall and told me if I ever come near his daughter again he'd kill me, and he means it, honest to God, Duff, he means it. That little old man had murder in his eye. Time I got my shoes on, he had dragged that kitchen table into the front yard and, right in front of his neighbors, he breaks it up with an axe and every swing he yells, 'Bastard.' I walk as fast as I can but I can hear the axe, blow after blow, and Archie yelling like that, 'Bastard! Bastard! Bastard!' I'm surprised you didn't hear about it. They say that table was nothing but toothpicks when he finally stopped. God, Duff, I don't think I can screw anymore. Every time I start to get a hard-on, I think of Archie and that axe."

At the end of the evening we shake hands at the post office and go our separate ways, Mouse to Riverside, me to Whitehall. The army will have its hands full.

Heather gets a four-day break at Christmas and I ask her to marry me. We set the date in June. She'll be away two more years for training but we'll have some weekends.

Lawrence helps me build an apartment in the basement of our house. The first thing we take out is the homemade boxing ring.

"God, it's solid. Your old man built this to last."

The ring posts are secured to the floor with bolts, the platform is two-by-fours and planking. The canvas is stretched tight. Working with crow bars it takes over an hour to rip the thing apart and carry the remains to Lawrence's truck.

"You want the ropes for a keepsake?" he asks.

"No."

As he drives away, one piece of rope dangles over the tailgate and keeps hitting the road. It's throwing punches back at me, bouncing jabs, one after another. The truck picks up speed and the rope ricochets higher, challenging me to one final round. The truck disappears and I sit on our front steps, realizing that I've just pried and tugged and torn apart my past.

28

DANNY

In May, a month before our wedding, Mouse shows up in the uniform of the Black Watch Highlanders and inspects our almost completed basement apartment, as if he were General Morrison reviewing the regiment. Everybody makes a big fuss over him. Heather calls him handsome and takes his picture by her maple tree. My mother makes him an apple pie. She is in a remarkable mood these days, delighted we'll be living downstairs. The need to furnish our place sharpens her natural ability as a bargain hunter.

"How can I tell her?" Heather asks as we examine the latest gift, a swan lamp. "She's so nice. I can't hurt her feelings."

"Maybe she'll get the message if we just put it away somewhere — like the furnace room."

"Duff, we can't do that."

The cost of converting the basement is more than I figured and I've taken another job. Between wiring houses and fishing, I'm mowing the fairways and greens at the Parrsboro Golf Club. Mouse wants us to go out all the time, a movie in Amherst or a weekend in PEI, but I'm saving as much as possible.

"At least come to Hank Snow," he pleads. He's flush with army pay and the money is burning a hole in his pocket. When I explain I need every cent I can get to buy a boat, he arrives with three tickets. "My treat," he says.

Hank Snow plays about once a year at the Parrsboro auditorium. It's a good pickin' and playin' town. Dusty Owens, from WWVA in Wheeling, West Virginia, shows up occasionally with a big circus tent, a band and a warm-up comic. Wilma Lee and Stoney Cooper also come to town. Of all the country music set, Hank Snow, the Singing Ranger, is the most frequent visitor. He packs the place. Cars and trucks are parked haphazardly along King Street. Hank's in town! Heather and I hold hands and Mouse, in uniform, walks in front of us.

"Does Mouse ever take that uniform off? He must press those pants wearin' 'em," Lawrence chuckles.

When I ask Mouse why he doesn't wear civilian clothes for a change, he says curtly, "Didn't bring any."

The show is set for eight o'clock and when we arrive at seven-thirty the auditorium is almost full. It's been a very warm day for late May and even with the windows open, the auditorium is hot. Heather and I sit there talking to people around us, while Mouse is in constant motion. He jumps up and down, greeting people, going out for a smoke, then back to his seat, then down the aisle and back again. By eight-thirty the show still hasn't started and people are getting restless. A small girl starts to cry and Mrs. John Cameron has to be helped outside, overcome by the closeness. At twenty minutes to nine Mouse rushes back to his seat.

"Guess what?" he says excitedly. "Hank is drunk. We just saw him being helped in the side door." The story spreads that Hank is walking on unsteady legs. Fifty minutes late, the show begins with a warm-up band. They play a long time. Finally Press Phinney yells, "Where's Hank?" Then Archie Durant yells, "Is he the Singin' Ranger or the missing ranger?" That brings a hoot from the audience.

When Hank finally appears he's decked out in a white suit with green sequins. He sings all his hit songs, about goin' down the track and not comin' back — lonely in jail and lost in love. He sounds just like he does on the radio, but for weeks the debate around Parrsboro is whether or not Hank Snow was drunk. It's the cause of a fist-fight Saturday night at Manning's dance. As the Mounties cart them off, one of the combatants, an inebriated Percy Pettigrew, yells out the window of the police car, "Let's hear it for Hank."

To which another inebriate in the crowd yells back, "Percy for fan club president."

At our place Heather is getting upset again.

"Maybe he was ill," she says. "I don't see why people keep picking on the poor man."

"Don't take it personally, Heather," Dewey says.

"I'm not taking it personally," she says a little too strongly.

Heather has repeatedly come to the defense of Hank Snow.

"Do you suppose it's because her father looked something like him?" Dewey asks.

"I don't know," says Curly, who has brought his own beer and is drinking it on our back porch. "But I'm not mentioning the subject again."

Heather reprimanded Curly two nights earlier for malicious stories about Hank and I wonder now if there is a connection with her father. She is very sensitive about anything to do with her father and lately her nerves seem frayed.

Dewey has finished his first year of college. His black hair is long and he's talking differently. He's my best friend, will be my best man, but old Dew is putting on airs.

"He's a college man now," my mother says.

"Does that mean he has to use 'actually' every second word? I thought college was supposed to broaden your vocabulary."

"It's just a phase."

My stag is planned for Dewey's house the first Saturday in June.

"God, it will seem like my going away party."

"All the same crowd except for Danny. He isn't coming."

"Did you invite him?"

"I invited him but he said he couldn't make it. It's Heather, isn't it? You took her away from him."

"But I didn't really."

"No, not really, but he feels he might have got her back if you hadn't come home."

"Maybe."

"No maybe, Duff. Danny feels you cut in on him and Heather."

"Maybe he should remember she went with me first."

Danny is taking a welding course in Halifax but often comes home. When you live in a town with a single main street you can't help but run into people. We had an awkward meeting one morning a month after I got home.

"Hi, Duff, heard you were home."

"How's it going, Danny?"

"Good."

"You like your course?"

"Yeah."

"Drop by sometime."

"Okay."

He doesn't drop by and Heather doesn't want him at the wedding.

"He's been one of the gang for a long time. If we don't invite him we'll look small and spiteful."

"I would rather not have him there," she says and I know she means it. When Heather is serious about something, her eyes almost close and her lips draw very tight.

"But why?" I ask, trying to understand her reasoning. "You went out with him, you broke up. Big deal."

She turns her back and mumbles something under her breath.

"What?"

"There's more to it," she says.

"Well, whatever there is, we have to invite him. Whether he comes or not is up to him."

Her face is flushed as she turns to me and there is a hint of rage in her voice. "Goddamn it, Duff, it's my wedding too!" She's up the stairs and slams the door. The vibrations run through our little apartment. The wedding has her in a tailspin, I tell myself, trying to restore some calm to the emotions running through me. As I stand there with the sound of the door still ringing in my ears, I hear his raspy voice. There are only two words, but they're his. "Be careful." There is nothing else. The apartment is silent.

"Women are never easy to understand," says Rob Davieson as we wire the Wasson house in Whitehall. We've been talking and he asks me about the wedding, maybe seeing something is wrong with me. I finally blurt out what happened this morning with Heather. I don't give him all the details, just that Heather was upset about wedding plans. He nods in a knowing sort of way.

"I've been married twenty years and my wife — " He stops as suddenly as he started, as though someone pushed a button inside him. We finish the day's work quietly.

Heather's mother, Mabel, is a woman filled with good cheer. She's a pack a day gal who cooks at Wheaton's and is always ready with a husky greeting and a smile. Tonight she isn't smiling.

"She's in the backyard and she's been crying for hours."

"Mabel, what's wrong?"

"I thought you must have had a fight. That usually happens just before a wedding."

Heather is sitting on the swing her father built for her the summer he drowned. She was fourteen and winter and summer the swing hangs off the big limb of their maple tree.

"When I feel alone," she told me once, "this is where I come."

Her back is to me and she's looking through the trees and across the old railway tracks to the water. A crooked moonbeam dances on the surface. When the tide is low our backyards face a muddy, empty ravine that twice a day fills with water and turns into a wide, wonderful salt water river.

She braces as I approach.

"Heather?"

The swing is barely moving. I stop the motion and turn her around. Her eyes are red and swollen.

"Heather, I had no idea you felt so strongly about this. We just won't invite him."

"It's not him, Duff, it's me."

"What do you mean, it's you?"

There is a long hesitation. Then she gets up from the swing and turns to me. "The first week you were home, after we'd made love in the field, Danny showed up in Halifax at the nursing residence. He pleaded with me to go for a walk with him. My head was spinning, I was so happy to have you back in my life. I guess I felt sorry for him. We walked down and sat on a bench in the Public Gardens. He told me he loved me, that he wanted me back. Duff, he cried and when I asked him why he waited until you showed up, he got mad.

Then he cried again. I could see he was sincere and . . . " She stops and turns towards the water.

"I took him in my arms and for a few seconds I didn't know anymore. I didn't know . . . " She pauses and cries again. "I didn't know Danny from you. I had doubts, Duff. For a few seconds I wasn't sure you were the one. It scared me but my doubts made Danny persistent. He didn't stop even after we announced our engagement. In Halifax he'd show up at my door whenever he felt like it. I told him no repeatedly and finally refused to see him. He still didn't stop until I complained to the security people at the nursing residence. Duff, Danny sometimes scares me. He's so, I don't know, persistent."

I take her shoulders and hope she can't feel the tremble running through me.

"Why would you keep this from me?"

"I didn't want you doing anything about it."

"You mean you didn't want me going after Danny?"

"Yes."

"He won't be coming to the wedding, Heather, and if he ever comes near you again — tell me."

"There's something else you better know," she says with a trembling voice.

"What?"

"I'm pregnant."

29

JAVIER TURNS HEADS

Heather slaps me hard when I ask if the baby is mine. "Goddamn it. It's your child but I'll call it all off if that's what you want." She walks over to kick a leafless rosebush and then walks away. Somewhat dazed and frankly upset that she has kept so much from me, I follow her down over the bank to the shore.

"The question is what you want. Better you go with Danny if he's your choice."

"That's not the choice. It's you or nobody. Danny touched my heart for a second but when I took him in my arms I knew — at that moment, I was absolutely certain, you were the only man I wanted. But can't you imagine how guilty I felt, the doubting — even for a second? I was scared and unsure. Then, on top of that, my period didn't come. Oh shit! Could anything else go wrong?"

We spend the night in each other's arms and I can feel a great relief in my bride-to-be. She has released her secrets and while I'm shaken she has kept so much from me, I realize she is a woman who doesn't let go of her feelings easily. We have weathered our first crisis. The baby will be born in six months.

The weeks before the wedding we talk of trust. I want to know why she keeps so much to herself. She hasn't trusted her feelings

142

since her father died. She thought he would always be there. Then it comes back to my father.

"You sometimes intimidate me with your enthusiasm. You're so much like your father it scares me."

"That's not all bad," I reply.

"It's not all good either," she says. "I was always afraid of your father."

"Most people were."

"Were you?"

"He could scare me, I guess, but it wasn't fear or intimidation that drove me. His enthusiasm was infectious, and he was my idol."

"He still is." There is no response from me.

Wedding plans are now in full swing between Heather, Mabel and my mother while all I can do is sit and listen.

"Kind of left out of things?" Lawrence snickers.

"There is not much for the man to do."

"Be glad about it," he says.

I've invited Javier and Manny to the wedding, not expecting either of them to come but I wanted to make the gesture anyway. With their invitations they're told a gift isn't necessary but I wanted them to know I'm thinking of them. I also told Manny — again — how much I loved the spy glass and I brought him up to date on my plans. He writes a one-page note, saying he's sorry he can't come and sorry to hear I'd lost the *Martha Jane*. He will keep my address and write again. There isn't a letter from Javier. Then one night the phone rings, and it's him.

"Maybe I come," he says.

"Really?"

"Yes really, maybe. I maybe come and look at Canada. Maybe opportunity there for me."

They've sold the big house, he tells me.

A week later he phones again to tell me he's definitely coming, flying to Montreal then Halifax. On his way home he's going to look around in Montreal where he has cousins.

"Bryson gets me a job in the same warehouse as you. I hate it. Make no good money and I hate it. Canada has good schools, maybe we come."

My mother hardly notices when I tell her a friend from Philadelphia will be staying with us.

"We'll have to vacuum the spare room," is her only reply. She doesn't ask who the friend is or anything. He could be Jack the Ripper, but the flowers have to be ordered and there is a problem with the carnations.

Javier arrives the day of my stag. At the Halifax airport he dances around and hugs me like a lost brother. With a wry smile Dewey looks him over. Javier is very excited.

"Man, man you look so good!"

On the way home he never stops talking.

"So much space, so much land!" It is a beautiful day and he's impressed.

When we arrive in Parrsboro, Javier instantly stamps his personality on everything. For starters, he hugs and kisses my flabbergasted mother while Dewey and I try to contain ourselves.

"You are so good to have me."

"Why, thank you, I'm — I'm sure," she says, trying to straighten her hair, tousled by his embrace.

Heather watches the hugs and kisses planted on my mother and tries to offer her outstretched hand as a defense. Javier shakes it, kisses it and then repeats the hugs he's just given my mother.

"He's incredible," she laughs.

My stag is set for nine o'clock. Dewey tells me to come early. Irene Hunter has been like a second mother to me. Since grade four I've spent a lot of time in her kitchen eating jam and peanut butter sandwiches. Even when the old man and Lloyd were squabbling, Irene and my mother remained friends. She is the soul of kindness and has always treated me like another son. I tell Javier I'll be back for him in half an hour and walk over to Dewey's.

He takes me into his father's little study. Lloyd is sitting behind his desk. Irene is there, standing beside him.

"Duff," she says, "you know how we feel about you so I'm not going to make a speech." She walks around and hugs me. "We wanted to give you something special for your wedding. We got you and Heather a traditional gift, but this is particularly for you, something to show how much we love you."

She looks at her husband. Except for yelling at my father in the ring in Moncton, Lloyd has always been a man of few words. He simply smiles and hands me an envelope. I look at Dewey and open it. It's a bill of sale for the catboat. My name is on it.

I'm speechless and Dewey is enjoying it.

"You've always loved that boat, Duff. Now it's yours."

I take both Dewey and his mother in my arms. "Thank you." I wonder if the tears between our faces are all mine.

My legs shake as I walk back home because I can see my new possession tied up on the shore. It's waiting to take me back on the water. If it wasn't the night of my stag I'd be going right now. My happiness is overwhelming.

Unfortunately, at my stag things are rather tense. For starters, my friends aren't so quick to take to Javier.

"He's the weirdest son-of-a-bitch I've ever seen," says Lawrence.

"Quite the boy," says Dewey after Javier holds forth on the legal system in Mexico.

Curly just looks at him in a dumbfounded way. "To be truthful, Duff, I can't understand a goddamn word he says."

Javier doesn't notice. He is in an intense state of anticipation and enjoying himself immensely. The real tension comes when — surprisingly — Danny shows up.

"I didn't think Danny would come," I whisper to Dewey.

"I asked him, Duff, didn't you want me to?"

"Well, yeah, I guess so, Dew, I just didn't think he'd show up."

Dewey pats me on the back. "I guess he knows he's lost her and that's that."

"Just keep him and Mouse separated," I say.

"Yeah," Dewey nods. "There's bad blood between those two."

At first Mouse and Danny stay clear of each other. There's enough people for them to talk to, but after a few beer they're a little vocal. Finally Mouse comes over and slaps me on the shoulder.

"She's got the best man, buddy, no question about that." The comment stops most of the talk. Only Javier can be heard expounding on something and doesn't notice.

I try to keep things on a light note. There are plenty of joke gifts and I start to open them, anything to break the tension. Suddenly I hear Frankie Henwood cry, "Stop it, you guys. Stop it!"

Mouse and Danny are grappling at the threshold of the living room. Danny takes a swing and clips Mouse squarely on the jaw, knocking the big guy into a group who grab but can't hold him. Partially regaining his balance, a wild Mouse lunges at Danny, swinging at the same time. Danny ducks the punch but can't escape the motion of Mouse's body and the two of them crash into Irene Hunter's forty-gallon aquarium. There is a crunch and crackle of breaking glass and then water everywhere. Fancy goldfish, red, orange and white with flowing silvery fins, are now skimming across the wooden floor of the Hunters' living room.

The water hits me on the ankles as a fish slides under the china cabinet. Everybody is giving orders.

"Get a bucket!" "Fill the sink!" "Oh my God! Grab that one!" "There's one under the table!"

"You stupid assholes," Frankie shouts as Mouse and Danny untangle themselves. Danny's elbow is cut and there is blood on Mouse's fingers. They have to look after themselves. Buckets and mops are now flying as wriggling goldfish are retrieved. They're put in the bathtub, but it's new water and Dewey doubts they'll live.

"Even goldfish can't stand that much of a change in water. God, what's Mum going to say?"

"Dew, I'm sorry," Danny says, standing in the bathroom doorway with a towel around his elbow.

"Me too," chimes in Mouse. Dewey is upset and I'm just plain angry.

"Plan to chip in for a new aquarium," I yell at them. "Goddamn it, you guys! This is my stag!"

"Sorry, Duff."

The next ninety minutes are used to repair the damage as best we can. Dewey keeps checking the bathtub to see if the fish are dead. We mop and sop up the water with all the rags we can find, even going to the neighbors for old towels. Javier is being very particular sweeping up the glass. There is little talking, just low muffled voices. The happiness is gone and the tension replaced by recrimination. Danny and Mouse swear to replace the shattered aquarium which Danny has covered with a blanket.

"Looks like a casket under that blanket," Curly observes.

"Yes," I say. "It does."

Irene and Lloyd stay out particularly late to give us the house. When they get home they go directly upstairs and Irene gets ready for bed. She decides to have a quick bath. She turns on the light in the hall, goes into the bathroom and bends over the tub to put in the plug. Then a living thing, like slimy jelly, squirms over her wrist. She almost loses her balance and falls in with the fish. When she finally turns on the bathroom lights and sees her prized goldfish, she shrieks. Running to her aquarium, she screeches and a long vibrating, "Deweyyy!!!" goes across the land.

We hear her half a mile away. After mopping up, we take the rest of the beer and a bucket of clams Johnny Atkinson had dug, and walk along the salt water below Dewey's house. Irene's sound is like the cry of a wounded animal travelling along the empty shore. We sit there in silence, as if breathing will reveal us. Then Mouse and Danny say it again. "Sorry, Dew, sorry, Duff."

"Shut up, the two of you," Frankie snaps.

In the moonlight we sit in a circle around a fire and the steaming bucket. The clams are cooking in seaweed and the sweet aroma envelopes us. Javier is quiet now, subdued by the events of the evening. The rest of us — Dewey, Frankie and Johnny, Lawrence, Mouse, Curly, Danny, and me — talk about our times together: the boxing club, the bouts, our opponents, high school dances, fishing, girls.

"Whatever happened to Bertha Brown, the one that used to walk like a sergeant-major?"

"Joined the army," Frankie answers, and we all laugh.

Our conversation is on the past, as if tonight had never happened. In the morning we will be apologizing. I'll go to Irene's early. Right now we are remembering the good times we shared in this little town on the banks of the Minas Basin. Walking back along the shore, the light of dawn is seeping over the eastern sky.

"Going to be a good day," says Lawrence.

Danny waits until he's alongside of me. No one is paying any attention when he puts his hand on my shoulder.

"I'm sorry, Duff." We walk on in silence. I know he's not talking about the aquarium.

Of the seven big goldfish, six survive. Mouse and Danny go to Amherst the next afternoon and purchase a new forty-gallon aquarium and a beautiful multi-colored goldfish. Lloyd puts a new piece of plate glass in the front of the broken aquarium. Now Irene has two. The new goldfish is called "Stag."

Dewey and I sit in my kitchen on my wedding day, waiting to go to the church. The sun has broken through the clouds but the air is humid after a morning rain. We hear someone coming down the stairs. Suddenly Javier stands in front of us and we're speechless. He's wearing a powder blue tux with a pink bow tie and around his waist is a wide, pink cummerbund. His shirt is white and trimmed with black frills.

"My friend, I am ready for your wedding."

"You most certainly are," says Dewey.

They come to our wedding. Reports back from the church say people started arriving forty-five minutes before the start of the service.

"With our track record, people think something is bound to happen," Dewey observes. "Who wants to miss something like Lawrence's wedding? They want a good seat, just as long as I'm not sitting behind them."

What happens at our wedding is Javier. He has every eye on him as he walks up the aisle to sit with my family. At the reception, he dances and the people of Parrsboro stare in wonder. He shakes like a man coming unglued. The more champagne he drinks, the more excitable his dancing. No one is having a better time. At one point he captures Curly and preaches on the great Latin fighters and Curly just keeps nodding as if he's understanding every word. Heather and I dance cheek to cheek. Curly spins Mabel around the floor and Frankie Henwood has a waltz with my mother. Mouse has maimed Peggy Skidmore by stepping on her foot during a foxtrot.

Helped into a chair, she says, "It's alright, Mouse, but I'm not dancing with you any more. I've only got one good foot to hobble home on."

Javier hugs us when we leave for our honeymoon.

"You have wonderful family and friends."

"Thank you for coming, Javier, it's better than the last time we parted."

"You are my friend, Duff. May happiness be with you."

Happiness is with me.

In the first months of our marriage we live on love because that's all we have. Quickly, money becomes a problem. Based on what I've saved from three jobs, I'll need eight years for a down payment on a scalloper. I work constantly, except the two weekends a month Heather is home. Those are times for us. That's why when there is a knock on the door Saturday afternoon I don't want to answer it, but Heather is too conscientious.

"There's someone for you."

A slightly balding, middle-aged man is standing there, in a sports shirt and slacks. He looks like a salesman.

"Hi, Duff, remember me?" He holds out his hand. "Leo Cormier."

If you know boxing you know the Cormier family. Two brothers are trainers and Leo is the most successful promoter in the Maritimes.

"Can I come in?"

"Of course, Mr. Cormier."

"Call me Leo."

"You know I'm not boxing anymore?" I ask him.

"I heard."

Over tea, Leo talks.

"You know Kid Carter?"

"Who doesn't?"

"I'll be honest with you, Duff. They feel Carter has another shot at a world title. His backers want him to meet some tough competition. He's fought the same guys, two, even three times. The ranks are a little thin in the middleweight division, as you know."

"Kid Carter needs seasoning," I say. "He's been Canadian middleweight champ for what, five years?"

"Six," he replies. "It's not seasoning so much as variety. He needs new guys to give him a challenge. There aren't that many middleweights who could go toe to toe with Kid Carter."

He puts his teacup in his saucer.

"I think you could." He pauses and I hear Heather's breathing stop. "And if you're interested, I think I could get the fight in the Maritimes, Halifax or Saint John maybe. You're known here and Carter is known nationally so it would be a good purse. A really good purse, Duff."

"Why would you ask me? I've never fought professionally except once in Philadelphia and I lost, got knocked out."

"I don't know what happened in Philadelphia but I've seen you fight and you're as good as anybody, including Kid Carter. You're certainly the only middleweight around Atlantic Canada who punches like a heavyweight. I can guarantee you a good payday."

"How good?"

"Twenty-five hundred dollars guaranteed, plus expenses while training. Good money, Duff."

"I'll think about it."

He isn't out of our driveway before Heather starts. "You aren't serious, you wouldn't go back in the ring?"

"No, I'm not serious. It's just if I had that kind of money, I could make the down payment on a scalloper. The bank will help me if I can help myself."

"That's even worse than boxing. I don't want you fighting and I certainly don't want you fishing." She fears the water above everything.

"Heather, I'm working at three jobs. There is so little to show for it and we've got a baby coming."

She sits the way she does when she's disturbed, her back rigid in the chair, looking straight ahead as if she's seeing something far, far away. I pace back and forth in front of her, in our small living room, convincing myself. I don't want to do it but it's the fast way, the quick way — just one fight, that's all we would need, just one.

30

GETTING READY

Sunday night Heather returns to Halifax and I go for a long walk on the beach. I'm reaching back and receiving the sounds I've grown up with — the low rumble of the receding tide, waves lightly slapping the wet sand. Two gulls are circling overhead, looking for something to eat. Little streams are running down the beach, chasing the vanishing water. My steps make deep impressions. I don't know why, but I put on my running boots, the five-pounders. Didn't really mean to wear them, I wasn't planning on running. Deep down, I still feel the way I felt in Philadelphia. Boxing is behind me, but it's a quick solution to a more satisfying life than wiring houses and mowing golf greens. Another reason nags at me tonight. This way, the old man's training won't be wasted. All those hours, all those years in the ring. His gift was in making me good enough to fight. Indirectly his gift will be my scallop boat. It's a satisfying thought. The sun is going down and the two gulls are now calling way out on the water. The next day I phone Leo Cormier.

We meet in the coffee shop at the Cumberland Inn in Amherst. Cormier is with his younger brother Arlie.

"I'll fight Kid Carter but I need more than twenty-five hundred. I need five thousand."

"Jesus, kid, that's more than I can handle."

"I'm sorry, Mr. Cormier."

"Call me Leo. Look, what if I can raise, say, three thousand? We can probably swing that."

"Sorry, it's five or nothing. I want to buy a boat and that's the down payment. I can't take less."

The Cormier brothers tell me all the reasons why I'm asking too much. Arlie is tougher than Leo and I immediately don't like him.

"For a fighter right out of the backwoods," he says, "with no pro experience, to fight a Canadian champ — I mean, my God, man, that's unheard of. What an opportunity for you and on top of it you're demanding five grand. That's almost as much as we have to pay Carter. Come on, be reasonable."

I get up.

"Sorry for wasting your time."

"Duff, listen."

"Leo, you came to me first and told me to think about it. Well, I thought about it. Unless you can guarantee me five thousand dollars free and clear I won't fight."

Four nights later he phones me back and offers four thousand. I refuse. The next night he calls again. "We've got a deal and you get your five grand."

Saturday I drive to Amherst and buy a new pair of boxing gloves.

Heather is shaken.

"Don't claim you're doing this for me or the baby. You were through with boxing. I want it behind you."

"Tell me how I can make five thousand dollars and put us on the road to a better life."

"We have a good life."

"Heather, you're not even going to be able to finish nursing. You'll be home with a baby and I'm an electrician's helper. How good will that be?"

"Good enough," she replies sharply.

She is impractical and argumentative. My mother is moody. She silently cries at her kitchen table.

"He wins. Even in the grave he's getting his way." She looks at me. "I'll give you the money for your boat, if that's why you're doing this. You can call it a loan."

"No thank you, Mother, I'm doing this on my own. Besides, you can't afford it."

"I've got this house. I can take a mortgage on it."

"No, I'll do this my way."

She puts her face in her hands. "You have your father's stubbornness, you know."

With the two women I love upset with me, I start roadwork.

Once again I'm around the four-mile square. The members of the Parrsboro Boxing Club are delighted.

"You'll put the town on the map. God, Kid Carter and Duff Martin," says Curly. He's close to dancing when he gets excited and he's jumping around in little steps. "I want to be one of your cornermen."

"Of course, Curly."

Leo Cormier is smart. He puts Frankie Henwood on the undercard. If Frankie wins, he'll go up the ranks in the light heavyweight division. Frankie and I spar everyday and the boxing club has more hustle and bustle than it's seen in years. St. Bridget's church hall is full of the whirl of skipping ropes and the rat-a-tat-tat of the small bag. Frankie has twenty-two pounds on me and he hits hard. Only my speed makes him work, but when he tags me it stings, turning my skin pink. Curly slaps some lotion on my red back and face, while humming a Jo Stafford tune, "See the pyramids along the Nile . . . " He is beside himself with happiness. The club is the way it used to be in the old man's days — noisy and active. When Frankie and I spar, usually a couple of rounds a day, Curly runs up and down the ropes, never sure who to cheer for, Frankie the light heavyweight or me the middleweight. Me, facing a longtime Canadian champ. Me, who threw his gloves in the garbage.

People from all over the county come to see us. They'll drop a nickel or dime in the contribution box by the door and stand around talking in low voices while we skip or spar. The biggest crowds come when Frankie and I spar. Mingled among men with lined faces are freckle-faced boys with wide eyes and runny noses. There is a smell of stale tobacco, engine grease and fresh wood chips. A few women visit. Eva, with rollers in her hair, is here everyday telling me to kick Kid Carter's ass. Lawrence is helping with the weights. He whispers, "I'd rather fight Kid Carter than Eva."

I train everyday, even when Heather comes home — there can be no letup now. She says she has come to grips with the fight and I believe she means it. She is beautifully pregnant and most passionate. She will complete her first year of training and take a leave of absence. The baby is due in late January. My fight with Kid Carter is set for Halifax, January fifteenth, 1959.

When I'm not training, I'm looking for a scallop boat. Lawrence and I make a couple of day trips, looking at prospects. I go through fishing regulations, meet the banker and look up licensing people in Halifax. Through it all, I'm happy. I can see a future.

My mother sees my future, face down in the ring with a sneering Kid Carter standing over me. She too has — grudgingly — relented. The first sign is a softening of her footsteps upstairs. She no longer clumps around, pounding her displeasure into the floorboards. Above all, she is a loving woman who cannot stay out of sorts for long. Her irrepressible spirit kept the old man's rambunctious personality from smothering her. Even with him, she could never stay upset. She brings me down an apple pie, some jam and a hug. Then leaving, she turns to tell me she wishes I was still her little boy again, so she could send me to my room. Soon, she has a new concern. Kid Carter is rude. He is quoted in the papers as saying he's coming to Nova Scotia to give a lesson to an upstart. He'll carry me for a few rounds before he bloodies my nose and sends me home crying.

"If you're coming to watch Dogpatch boy take the middleweight championship, stay home. If you're coming to see me humiliate one of your locals, then come."

"He's trying to bait the public, the jerk," says Heather. It seems to have worked — the Halifax Forum is full.

After much soul-searching Heather is here, sitting in the front row next to Leo. My mother is at home.

"You know I cannot go. I cannot bear to see you hurt. Beat him, Duff, but don't hurt him."

Every fighter has secrets, a unique training procedure that gives him an edge. The last few days before a fight, I do roadwork in my heavier boots. The five-pounders are replaced with ten-pounders. That's a lot of lead to lug around the four-mile square. The pay-off comes when I'm ready to get in the ring. In light boxing shoes I can almost fly. Besides roadwork and taking stinging punches from

Frankie, I've been using thirty-pound dumbbells. If my arms ache when I'm finished, I think of our baby, a new boat, our better life. I hit the big bag, hard. Again and again I hit it hard. I am my old man's son.

Frankie wins a close decision. He is mauled in the early rounds but stays with his man and beats him on points. Leaving the ring, Frankie's face is red, his bottom lip puffy and both eyes are almost closed. All he can manage is a weak, sweaty hug and "Go get 'em."

We are the main event and Leo is edgy. "Give him a good fight, Duff, that's all I ask. Give him a good fight. People want the main event to be a scrap. They don't think you've got a chance but I do. Just be careful, this guy is cagey as hell."

Leo has taken a lot of criticism for this fight. The press has never been positive. Sports writers wonder why a Canadian champion is fighting a Maritimer with no professional standing. They suggest Carter is just trying to puff up his knockout record. When questioned, Leo is cool.

"If Kid Carter wants an easy win, he wouldn't agree to fight the best middleweight in the Maritimes."

I'm in the ring waiting and Carter gets a chorus of boos as he walks down the aisle. The biggest noise is coming from a solid block of Parrsboro fans, four school buses full. They are particularly vindictive to him. One of the Welton boys holds up a sign, "From Dogpatch — Carter is Dogshet."

"Would have been better if he could spell shit," says Curly.

"He gets 'T' for trying," chuckles Lawrence.

The Parrsboro section starts a chant as the Welton boys correct their spelling.

"Duff, Duff, Duff, Duff, Duff."

This is what was missing in Philadelphia. I tighten my glove and bring it up to my face. I stare into the leather.

I'm ready.

The Fight

Kid Carter, meeting thousands of boos and jeers, climbs through the ropes. I saw him for the first time at the weigh-in this afternoon. He's older looking than twenty-six. His nose has a dent in it, the calling card of a tough fight. He smiles at the boos but gives me a dirty look, twisting his upper lip into a sneer.

Sitting close to ringside, Heather blows me a kiss. I'm not afraid of Kid Carter.

We're standing in the middle of the ring as the ref gives his instructions. I'm in black trunks and a new white terry cloth robe with the Parrsboro Boxing Club on the back, a gift from Lawrence and Curly. After the fight, I'm going to donate it to the club.

Carter is in gold robe and trunks. His cornermen are in gold shirts with "Kid Carter" on the back. They're a contrast to my guys. Lawrence's red hair is going every which way, a corner of his wrinkled white shirt hanging out of his pants, his stomach overflowing. He's a man about to burst. Next to him is cross-eyed Curly. Standing next to Lawrence, he's a puny runt in a wrinkled shirt, baggy pants and sneakers. Nope, it isn't Kid Carter's corner, but I'm grateful they are who they are, and I'm glad they're here.

"What's so funny?" Lawrence asks.

"You guys. I'm glad you guys are my cornermen."

Curly smiles, "Beat him, Duff. Beat the son-of-a-bitch. Beat him for Alex."

This is not a title fight. I will not become Canadian champ if I win, but I will still have won. Curly's words are in my head as the bell rings.

"Beat him, Duff."

Kid Carter turned pro at nineteen. He's had fifteen professional fights and a dozen knockouts. He's never lost and I quickly see why: his punches sting. We start off with solid jabs. He learns quickly I can counterpunch. By the end of the first round, he knows this is not a cakewalk. Round two has him changing his stance, crouching more, already looking for a power punch. There are good blows by both of us; the crowd is into it. I'm looking for a weakness. At the end of the second round, I ask Curly, "Do you remember the old man talking about the bob-too, how some fighters move their heads with their fists?"

"You seeing that in him?"

"Just in his combinations, and not all the time either, but twice with his first punch in a combination, he bobbed his head with his punch."

"Can you nail him?"

"I don't know. He's good. If I can just take my time."

In the third round I land a solid hook on Carter's jaw. He staggers, but comes right back. He has stamina and he's fast — not as fast as Juan, but fast enough.

"You're doin' well but he's hitting you a lot under your eye."

Curly is applying pressure below my right eye where a small welt is starting to swell. I've split Carter's lip and his corner is trying to stop the bleeding. After three rounds, I'm still toe to toe with him.

"Watch for that combo," says Curly as the bell signals round four, "and keep up your guard. Keep him off that eye."

The old man used to tell me, "Don't let the fight get into a pattern, be unpredictable, never let your opponent get used to you." I change my footwork and start using my left.

In the middle of the round, I get him with a right cross and hit him hard enough to momentarily stun him. He tries to get back in the fight with his — yes, his combination, and wait for it, wait for it.

Here it comes — the right and the head bobbing slightly ahead and down. And I nail him! As hard a punch as I've ever thrown. A right hook with all my body into it. The impact runs up my arm like an electric current. Kid Carter, Canadian champ, seeker of a world title, staggers, one foot ahead of the other, his guard down. I throw another punishing right. The pain is awful; my arm, elbow and shoulder are on fire. I don't need anything more. Carter takes another wobbly step, tries to focus, and falls.

People said you could hear the Parrsboro fans all the way back to town, a hundred and twenty miles away. They were jumping in the aisles, running up and down, climbing into the ring, indignant to Carter who is just coming around.

"How about Dogpatch now?" Arnie Cochrane yells.

The reporters are all over us and refuse to believe I'm not offering Carter a rematch, with his title on the line.

"You're twenty, and you're retiring?"

"I'm not boxing anymore. This was for only one fight and I've had it."

Curly and Lawrence stand next to me, happy with the win, glum at my comments. My dressing room is full of Parrsboro fans. There's hardly room for Heather to give me a victory kiss. She knows it is over. We have a pact. A bond between us. I will stop fighting and she will stop protesting my life, working on the water.

"Maritimer beats champ and retires at twenty," reads the headline in the *Montreal Gazette*. The *Toronto Telegram* reports, "Kid Carter knocked out by a nobody." The press pictures me as an oddball, turning my back on fame and money. Most people agree.

"I don't want you looking like Kid Carter," my mother says as Heather nods in agreement.

How can I explain it to them? It isn't what I'll look like; it's deeper than that. I knew that night in Philadelphia I was through with boxing. A championship was the old man's dream and it was something I was not going to pursue.

My victory doesn't give me peace. Kid Carter is furious, not a gracious loser. He's demanding a rematch and calling me yellow. His excuse is he didn't train for the fight because he thought I wasn't much of a fighter. Well, he says, he was right, I am not much of a fighter. Just a cowardly nobody who got in one lucky punch.

"Mr. Lucky Punch," he snarls in the press.

All three Cormier brothers come to my house.

"The sky's the limit, Duff."

"I know, but . . . "

"Please, Duff."

"Leo, I fought him and that's it."

Within a month I buy the thirty-two foot scallop dragger the *Nancy & Myrtle*. It's bad luck to change the name of a boat, which is too bad, because a week after I take possession, a pink, howling Virginia Dawn is born.

32

THE RIP

The *Nancy & Myrtle* proves to be a worthy vessel but in the next two years the price of scallops takes a nosedive. I earn extra money fishing flounder and Lloyd Hunter sells me one of his lobster licenses. We aren't rich but we're happy and have hopes for the future. At night we talk about building our own house and having more children. I'm never tempted to go back in the ring. Boston, Philadelphia and even Kid Carter seem long ago.

Virginia is the light of our lives. Sometimes I go into her room while she's sleeping and just watch her. Awake, she is constant motion with a bouncy personality and her mother's blond hair. She also has a new playmate. Lawrence and Agnes have a baby girl, three months younger than Virginia. She's as tiny as Agnes but as Curly says, "She's all Lawrence."

"Agnes calls her Freda," Lawrence says. "What the hell kind of a name is that?" He wants Mary or Joan or Jane but relents and immediately starts calling her Freddie. He even calls Virginia Ginny, and much to Heather's objection, it's catching on.

Freddie and Ginny are fast friends. You can't miss them, running down the beach. The light bounces off Freddie's golden red curls and Ginny's almost white hair.

160

Ginny has my love of the water and Heather is now determined to overcome her own fears. She is reading books on facing the things that scare you. One day, she leans over and kisses me during lunch.

"I'm ready."

"You sure?"

"Yes."

We start sailing. Sunday excursions up and down the Minas Basin. Ginny keeps Heather so occupied she hardly has time to be nervous. It's when Ginny falls asleep in her arms that Heather has to calm herself. I love her for this, because she's really trying, gulping down her fear and putting a smile on her frozen face. She's doing it for Ginny and me.

Dewey brings his new girlfriend to Parrsboro the weekend before Mouse ships off for three years in Germany. We have a picnic on the beach at Port Greville. Curly, the Henwood brothers, Agnes and Freddie go with Lawrence in the *Fundy Mist*. Dewey takes his girlfriend, my mother and his parents and a few neighbors in one of his father's boats. Heather and Ginny and I leave early and sail the catboat. It's the first time I've seen Dewey in almost six months and I'm happy to see he's stopped saying "actually" and using sentences peppered with "one must" or "one does."

Frankie Henwood is home for a week. He is a professional boxer now, fighting out of Montreal.

"That Marie," Mouse says, taking a big swig of beer while looking at Dewey's girlfriend. "She has an outstanding ass."

"Mouse!" Heather scolds, and to get him off the track of Marie's curves I ask,

"How's your love life, Mouse?"

He scowls, "Not good. I was hot to trot for this waitress near Camp Gagetown. We went out, had fun, and then I meet her husband. Seems she forgot to tell me she was married."

"Poor Mouse," Heather says, putting her hand around his arm.

He looks at her. "If only you had a sister."

"God, Mouse, that would makes us brothers-in-law."

"Okay with me," he says.

We make a fire on the beach and cook a bucket of clams. Dewey has his guitar and we sing, talk, eat and supervise the construction of a sand castle. Irene Hunter has brought a bottle of wine. There is plenty of laughter.

"It's just a grand afternoon," my mother says, moving around people, trying to escape Curly, who has been telling her about his trip to Montreal.

"We'll have to wait awhile to get into the harbor," Dewey says as we pack up.

"Yeah, it will take a while. I'm taking Heather and Ginny across the bay and we'll follow the tide in."

"Drop over tomorrow night," I tell Dewey and Marie. Curly hears and says he'll come too. He tells Lawrence and Agnes and Freddie.

"Everybody come," says Heather, laughing. "We'll eat outdoors, if the weather's good."

Back on the water, we sail across the basin. It's the long way home but we have to wait for the tide anyway before we can get to the Parrsboro wharf. Ginny is already asleep and the late afternoon is beautiful. We talk about the people at the picnic.

"Marie seems very nice," Heather says, holding Ginny.

"Yes," I reply. "I noticed you two seem to hit it off. She was a big hit with Mouse. I thought his eyes were going to roll out of his head every time he looked at her."

"Mouse always seems so lost," she says.

"Too bad you didn't have a sister."

"I think the woman Mouse marries will always have her hands full."

"Mouse tells me he's been boxing in the army. Got a record of two and two. Both wins were technical knockouts and so were his losses."

"Poor Mouse."

"It's what the old man always told him — you can't win with poor defense, no matter how hard you can punch."

"It's nice what Frankie did for Curly, paying his way to Montreal," she says.

Frankie bought Curly a train ticket so Curly could go to Montreal and watch Frankie fight. It was all Curly talked about.

"Frankie's spending money like it's going out of style. I hope he knows the paydays don't last."

"Duff, I'm so happy with you."

She says things like that out of the blue. They always send a happy little vibration through me. I trim the sail and tack parallel to the sheer cliffs of Cape Blomidon. Heather closes her eyes. She is sitting in the middle of the deck, her back resting against the mast. Ginny is fast asleep in her arms.

"Heather! Look."

On the cliff high above, a small deer is trying to pick its way along the top of the bluff. It is directly above us, walking unevenly over the loose rocks.

"Oh, Duff, the camera. In my bag by your feet."

As I bend over to get the camera, Ginny wakes and follows her mother's gaze to the top of the bluff.

"Daddy, will it fall?"

"Oh no," Heather gasps as the young deer loses its footing near the edge, scrambling back just as unearthed rocks tumble down the steep cliff face.

"Daddy, is it hurt?"

"No, Ginny, it's alright," I reply.

She leaves her mother's arms and on unsteady feet runs to me with open arms. "Is it alright?"

"Yes, dear, it's fine."

The loose rocks are still falling. Hundreds of feet they cascade down the rock cliff, startling sparrows and gulls whose complaint is a crescendo of muted cries along the massive cliff.

I hold Ginny against me, drying her tears and telling her things are okay. "Why did it almost fall?"

"There are loose rocks up there."

On Ginny's insistence, I tack around to see if we can spot the deer again. She's still asking questions when a sharp wind catches the sail. Then I hear it — the rip. No longer confined by the rocky cliffs, millions of gallons of water, pushed and pressured by the incoming tide, pour out of shallow Scots Bay into the broader and deeper basin channel as if someone had squeezed a plastic bottle, forcing the liquid out in a rush. It's in this rip that I nearly lost the catboat years ago when I was learning to sail. Of all places on earth, this is where I should have been paying attention, not been distracted by a deer or even an upset daughter. Manny told me once that every sailor has a spot in the sea where he's closer to danger than any other place. "Your own personal hell hole" was the way he put it. I tell Ginny to go back to her mother. Just as she starts, another gust pulls the catboat. The deck goes up at a steep angle and Ginny stumbles against the gunnels, and with her face full of fear, tumbles over the side.

"Duff. My Jesus, Duff!"

"Heather, take the wheel."

We're moving faster and the noise of the rushing water is louder. I'm trimming hard against the stubborn wind but it catches the bow and pulls us into the outside waters of the rip. The current carries us into the faster water and the little catboat spins violently.

"Heather, take the wheel!" She is white and frozen. "Oh, Jesus. Heather, please!"

The water is roaring and suddenly a great swell pushes us sideways, arching the deck perpendicular to the swirling foam.

The deck levels off as the boat is flung away from the torrent. I don't bother trying to turn. I drop anchor and run to the bow, screaming Ginny's name. I hear her.

I'm in the water, swimming and crying out. Where? Where is she? Through the waves I see her white hair. She is flailing, fifteen feet in front of me. Then she's gone. The surface is all water, green, black-blue with white foam. I don't notice how much of it I'm swallowing. My heart is pounding so hard it's going to explode. Oh, God! On the second dive I see her, still wildly kicking and flailing under the surface. That wonderful white hair is just below me and I grab it. She is hysterical, slapping and scratching and crying.

"Mummy, Mummy, Mummy."

I have to reach the catboat. I have to!

"Heather." My voice and Ginny's crying mingle with the roar of the rip. She is uncontrollable and impossible to hold. The catboat is drifting, despite the anchor.

"Please, God. Oh, God, please, please! Heather, Heather. Help us."

I start to retch, I've swallowed so much water. I'm gasping for air so hard my stomach contracts and I'm spewing the picnic lunch over myself and my hysterical daughter. The sour vomit floats around us and Ginny continues to thrash.

The catboat is ten feet in front of us. On, on, on — I grab the bow rope but can't pull us up. Ginny is now crying softly, cold and bewildered.

I swim around the boat looking for a way to get us aboard, still calling Heather. Finally, with all I've got, I grip the anchor line, then the gunnel and heave Ginny on the deck. It takes me a minute to pull myself up. Heather is bending over Ginny and touching her, but her hands are shaking violently. I embrace her to try and stop her trembling. She strokes Ginny's hair in a very strange way. I get a blanket. Ginny is shivering and coughing. We're both spitting up seawater. I hold her in my arms and rub her. She cries softly as I take off her wet clothes and wrap her in the blanket. Heather watches and weeps. Finally in a broken voice she says, "I hate the water. Hate it, hate it, hate it! Every night I fall asleep hating it. Do you under-stand?"

The sun is setting. I try to hold them both. Above their sobs I hear an approaching engine. Coming through the sunset is Lawrence in the *Fundy Mist*.

33

B LACK AND W HITE

"Your daughter will be fine. She's just tired and your wife has had a traumatic shock." That's the way a fatherly Dr. Hill puts it. He is our family doctor, now in his seventies with a full head of snowy white hair. He looks me directly in the eye. "She needs to rest for a few days, I'll give you a prescription for her."

Ginny is upstairs in my mother's spare bedroom, which is just as well because when Heather wakes up, she is furious with me.

"Why didn't you bring her to me? Instead, you let her try and run back to me when the boat was moving and the deck was unsteady. How careless can you be? You just about caused her death, Duff. You know that?"

"I didn't know the boat was going to pitch at that very moment, Heather."

"But you should know, you're the sailor."

The tension between us spreads upstairs. Big Bobby Dowe gets a little lippy today. He is sent twice a week by his mother for extra help with English composition because he is in danger of failing. He tells my mother Shakespeare and Tennyson are dead and as far as he's concerned, they should stay that way. A startled Bobby can't answer back as my mother looks him straight in the eye and says,

"Wherefore, unlaurelled Boy,
Whom the contemptuous Muse will not inspire,
With a sad kind of joy,
Still sing'st thou to thy solitary lyre?
Do you want to spend your life bumming cigarettes on the post office steps, Bobby? Unemployed, a missed opportunity in a world of opportunities?" Before he can answer, she starts again.

"The melancholy winds
Pour through unnumbered reeds their idle woes:
And every Naiad finds
A stream to weep her sorrow as it flows."

"Bobby won't be back," she tells me later. "By now he's probably thrown Tennyson, Keats and George Darley off the Whitehall bridge." Her hand sweeps test papers off the kitchen table. I stoop and pick them up. "I'm sorry," she says.

"Yes, I know. It's all right."

"No, it's not all right. I'm failing that boy. Chesterton was right when he said a teacher who is not dogmatic is simply a teacher who is not teaching."

"He has to want it, Mother. He has to want something. You're going to lose some of them, you know that."

"Yes," she says, "I know that."

There comes a time when roles change. The parent who has always looked after you needs some looking after themselves. I know this is that time. When I put my arms around my mother, she doesn't want to let me go.

My wife, however, won't even let me put my arms around her.

Heather sits in our small living room, brushing Ginny's hair. "I want you to sell that catboat, or give it back to Lloyd or burn it. Just get rid of it."

I look at her, stunned.

"I mean it, Duff. If you keep it, Ginny will always want to go with you and I swear I'll never let her take another step in a boat. That boat or any boat."

"You know that boat means a lot to me, Heather."

"Does it mean more than me?"

167

Sitting on driftwood in the early evening, I see Dewey coming down the beach. He sits next to me. It's all over town about Ginny falling overboard.

"But it's all right, Duff, you saved her."

"Not quite all right," I answer. "Heather hardly speaks to me and she wants me to get rid of the catboat."

"Put it up by our place. After a while, things will cool down. She'll be all right." Dewey pauses. "Why don't you take Heather and Ginny on a little trip? Spend a few days in Halifax, get out of here for a while."

"Why are we going to Halifax?" Heather asks.

"Just for a trip."

"Can we afford to spend three nights at the Lord Nelson?"

"Is there animals to see?" Ginny wants to know.

The first day we walk in the Halifax Public Gardens or stroll along Barrington Street, stopping for a snack in the Green Lantern Restaurant and looking at the marquees at the Paramount and Capital theatres.

Abbot and Costello are playing at the Paramount. The short features the Three Stooges and Ginny loves it. I cast glances at Heather. She seldom even smiles.

The next day we buy Ginny a pair of shoes at Eaton's. Then we try something new, Chinese food. Ginny wants to go on a ferry ride to Dartmouth but Heather is adamant. "No, you're not going." Ginny starts to cry and Heather wants to go back to the hotel. On the way I buy Ginny a coloring book. We sit in the room trying out the new colors while Heather has a nap. After an hour, Ginny is restless and still wants to go on the ferry.

"No," I say. "Mummy doesn't want us to."

"But why?"

"Because you almost drowned and Mummy is worried, I guess."

Finally, we leave a note and slip out of the room. We walk in the Public Gardens again and have an ice cream. When we get back to the room, Heather is sitting up in bed.

"You took her, didn't you? You went on that ferry."

"No, we didn't," I say, laughingly. Although I can see by her eyes this isn't funny.

"Mummy, we had an ice cream," Ginny says.

Ignoring her, Heather's half closed eyes are on me. It's almost a snarl when she says, "Keep her away from the water."

Driving home the next morning, Ginny colors in the back seat. Heather and I hardly speak. The trip hasn't helped. In fact, it seems to have pulled us even farther apart.

I work the scalloper hard and I try to keep my spirits up. Fishing isn't what it used to be. The catches are down. The scallop beds are shifting. Even with higher prices, I'm making less than I did a year ago. One night, after a particularly hard day, I make the mistake of complaining. It brings more words out of Heather than she's said to me in a week.

"Give it up. Get out of it. Sell the scalloper and get a land job like other people. You don't need to be on that boat. Give it up." Her tone is sharp and unsympathetic.

Depressed, I walk along the beach. I've put the catboat in back of Dewey's place. If Heather sees me sailing past our house, she'll be furious. They say if it rains, it pours. My life is very wet lately.

Heather and my mother are out one evening when the doorbell rings.

"If you don't want me here, Duff, just say the word and I'm gone."

Leo Cormier always looks as if he dresses in the dark. Nothing matches. A big man, his light brown hair is always cut and combed just so. It's his clothes. He's wearing a blue raincoat, a green shirt and brown slacks that look like he slept in them. He owns a couple of racehorses and a small apartment building, yet he always looks down on his luck.

"Come in, Leo."

He sits in the same chair he did almost three years ago, and pretty much says the same things he said then.

"Kid Carter still wants another shot at you. You're the black mark he wants to erase. Undefeated except for you and Gene."

Carter, after much whining, was finally given a world title shot. He lost to Gene Fulmer's famous right hand.

"Duff." Leo gives me his serious look. "You're the fighter who knocked him out. Outside of the world champ you're the only one, and the fact you wouldn't give him a rematch always burned him. He wants a rematch with you and another shot at a world title and he'll

169

retire. Hell, it's his last shot. He's twenty-nine. He wants to leave a winner. Ya know something else? Secretly, I think Kid Carter admires you. He'll never admit it but I think he does."

"I haven't been in the ring in almost three years, Leo. I'm out of shape."

Leo is on his feet, pacing now.

"You're still young and strong and," he pauses, "you're the best there is, better even than Kid Carter. Give it serious thought, Duff."

Boxing? Back in the ring? Why does the idea suddenly have some appeal? Is this the diversion I need? We talk for an hour and Leo lays it out. A rematch in Montreal. A top purse and this time, Carter will put his title on the line.

"You could have it all."

"Leo, I don't know why I'm even sitting here thinking about boxing."

Leo's thin lips turn into a smile.

"You just have to give me a little time to think this over."

"Don't take too long, Duff. We'd want the fight this spring."

I don't sleep that night but that's not unusual. Shortly after the accident Heather put a folding cot in Ginny's room and sleeps there. I know she won't forgive me if I go back in the ring. I know it. So why am I doing this? Please God, what is driving me? What is it? I don't understand. "Come on," I hear him say. "Come on, get a hold of yourself. Come on, push."

As the first rays of the sun peep over the eastern sky I start around the four-mile square.

34

LONG TERM

The way Curly tells it, he opened the sports section of the *Halifax Herald* and dropped his coffee into his lap. "Damned near burned my balls," he says, holding the page with the pictures of Kid Carter and me with a story Leo leaked before the contracts are even signed. Curly is now hopping around my kitchen, as if the coffee is still burning his crotch. He is talking constantly, wanting to be my cornerman, wanting to help me train, talking so fast that Heather, after offering him tea, escapes. Curly is happy — she is not.

"Why would you do this? Haven't you put us through enough? How could you do this to us? You promised me you wouldn't go back in the ring."

"What could I do that would make you happy?"

"Keep your promises," she screams. "Keep our daughter away from the water. Keep away from boxing. Why are you doing this? To punish me? Is that why?"

"I don't know. Maybe I'm depressed and need something. A distraction, I guess."

I know it isn't much of an explanation. I can't answer her with anything logical. I go over how I felt in Philadelphia. I don't feel the old man's pressure anymore and maybe that's it. Maybe I still need a

171

connection with him. All I know is there's something in me that's missing.

"Is it because I asked you to stop sailing? Is that why?"

"No, sailing has nothing to do with it."

"Is it because I don't sleep in our bedroom, or because I want you to stop fishing? Is that it?"

I hear my words bounce off our kitchen walls. "Stop fishing, stop sailing. You want me to stop living! I can't stop living just because you're scared of everything."

"I'm not scared of boxing. I just hate it and I've got plenty of reasons to be afraid of the water," she cries. "They brought my father's body back to our house and set it on our kitchen floor. That's where I saw him, on our floor. He was soaked, his clothes sticking to him. He was white, like the color had been bleached out of him and pieces of seaweed were still sticking to him. His feet were bare and a tiny little crab was still on his pant leg." She lowers her voice. "Why would they bring a man to his family like that? I guess they didn't know any better. They stood around him, murmuring, waiting for the undertaker. My mother's crying woke me up and I came downstairs. There he was."

"I know it was awful, but you make it sound like it happened last week. It was years ago, Heather, years ago."

The entire conversation is in front of Curly. He puts his face in the newspaper and pretends he hears nothing. Afterward, Heather grabs her coat and goes to her mother's. Curly puts the paper down. He knows our house well. He goes into the den and takes down the photograph of the old man with Joe Louis. He brings it out to the kitchen.

"He'd be so proud, Duff." His eyes don't leave the photo. "You. middleweight champ! We always knew. Your old man, Lawrence and me, Frankie and Mouse, we always knew."

"Curly, my wife and my mother are so against this. I don't even know why I considered it."

"Because your old man spent the best part of his life getting you ready, that's why."

"But I'm not ready. Kid Carter is training his ass off. He figures he slipped up last time, didn't do enough preparation. That's not going to happen again. He knows this is close to the end of what has been a remarkable career."

"Bullshit," says Curly. "You'll beat him and I want to be with you. Even if I have to pay my own way to Montreal. I want to be there for you and," he shakes the photograph at me, "for Alex."

Leo and I immediately disagree. He wants me training in Moncton where suitable sparring partners are available.

"You need top-notch boxers who can give you a good work out."

I want to train in Parrsboro, until the end of the fishing season anyway.

"Train here, Duff. It's good for the club."

After Curly and I talk things over, he takes Ginny out to the back yard and I go upstairs to talk to my mother. She is outraged. "Mad as hell" is the way Lawrence puts it. I stand next to her at the kitchen sink and we watch Curly and Ginny walking in our back yard, hand-in-hand. Watching them, I expect Curly is explaining the characteristics of a good left hook to my daughter. Ginny just nods in amazement, trying to watch both Curly's eyes at the same time.

My mother watches. "That man. Half nervous tics and half dense. I suppose it's too bad he doesn't have anybody and here's you with so much and prepared to throw everything away. You're just like Alex and that's too bad."

"You're being hard on both of us."

"Am I? Look at that man out there. He was your father's best friend and I doubt his IQ is any bigger than his collar size."

"You underestimate Curly. He may not know the best lines in literature but he knows the best left hooks in boxing. He's not stupid. Are you sure you're not belittling him because of the way he looks?"

"Duff Martin, I have never belittled anyone because of his physical characteristics. Curly Dickie has been hanging around here almost since the day your father and I were married. I've never said an unkind word to him. I couldn't count the times he's had meals here and you have the nerve to say that."

When Dewey comes home for the weekend I get it again.

"How come?"

"You mean the boxing?"

"You know very well I mean the boxing. How come you're going back in the ring? I admit it, Duff, I'm damned surprised."

"Well, Dew, to tell you the truth, so am I. I really don't have an answer. Boxing is there, I guess. I know that's kind of dumb."

"It's not only dumb, it's very short term. So you beat this guy maybe, what then? You fight again and win and again, but it's still short term. What about after boxing?"

"You're way ahead of me, Dew. I can't get past tomorrow and you're talking long term."

"You need something long term. If the scallop beds are going, as they say, you'll need some kind of work. There aren't any old boxers."

He decides to run with me but can't keep up. "I'll see you tonight," he says, winded, as I leave him by the side of the road, half way around the four-mile square. That evening, first in Wheaton's and then in Burke's, we talk about my future.

"Let's both think about it over the next few weeks and find something you'd like to do."

"Even if fishing is bad, I'd like to do something with boats, that's all I know."

"That's a start."

Almost three years without weights or roadwork has turned me soft around the middle.

Leo puts an old guy named Jerry McPhee against me. He's no Kid Carter and way past his prime but he's a bulldog with a concrete head. He hits hard and slams lefts and rights into me. It takes all I've got just to keep up with him.

"God, Leo, maybe I shouldn't be doing this. That guy nearly had me."

"It's concentration, Duff. You're still rusty but it's coming back. We've got two months, you'll make it."

"Kid Carter has never been out of training. He's working like hell. How do I ever catch up to him?"

"It's not just physical, Duff, it's instinct. You've got great instincts in the ring. It's still there inside you. You just have to bring it out."

Driving back to Parrsboro I think about instinct. It's a word the old man drilled into me. Reading an opponent is like reading a book. There is a cover, a preface, a first chapter, the body and the end. The cover is the guy's reputation. The preface is the sneer he gives you when he enters the ring, the attitude during the ref's instructions. The first chapter is his opening round, whether he's going to carry the fight to you or let you carry it to him. The body is the middle rounds, when the fight develops a pattern and the end, the end is when you finish it. Read every part. Most fights are lost by a failure to read. "Sometimes," he used to say, "it's not really your opponent you're trying to beat but your own limits."

I test my limits. Heather is testing her patience. I have signed a contract. I cannot stop.

"Even if I leave you and take Ginny?"

"Please, Heather, don't say such things. Just let me get this fight over."

"No, there'll be another. And then another."

"No, there won't. I promise."

She startles me by suddenly laughing, a mocking laughter, insincere and challenging.

"I don't believe you. I don't even believe you can stop. Your father is stuck so far inside you, it's him I'm married to. Isn't it, Duff? It's him I'm with. He's the father of my child. You'll be hobbling around, an old man needing help to get through the ropes and you'll still be going in the ring."

Her words keep coming back to me. In my sleep I roll over to put my arms around her and she's not there. The next night I get up and go to her.

"Forgive me," I ask and kiss her lightly on the cheek. She opens her eyes and looks at me. Her voice is flat.

"There is nothing to forgive. I married you thinking I'd spend my life with you. I was wrong. I'm spending it with your father. Go back to bed, Duff."

If you're running up Western Avenue, Kirk Hill looms ahead of you at the halfway point on the four-mile square. In a gray, wet dawn it stands like a black hull coming out of the early morning darkness. It distracts me in one of those rare moments when I think I almost have it, that obscure, frustrating reason. Sometimes it's almost in my grasp. Then it goes again, slips away. I think deep, deep, deep down, that Heather is right. It's still got to do with him. It's him drawing me back to the ring — or is it me? Using him as my excuse. Or is it both of us? Because we are both of us. Somewhere off in the distance I hear an owl. Then there is just the sound of my feet. I wonder what ever happened to Wally the whale. How long do whales live? It's 5:20 a.m.

3 5

L E O

The big punching bag in the Parrsboro Boxing Club has been hanging there for fifteen years and it's never gotten the work out I give it. People stand around watching as I spend ninety minutes at a time, throwing hard punches. My shoulders pain and Curly gets concerned.

"Jesus, Duff, don't overdo it."

We've got more problems with Leo. He wants his own people in my corner. He doesn't like Curly and wants his people handling me. Leo can be stubborn, even brutish, but he's not pushing me around. I'm not afraid of him and I've got a lot of the old man in me with my own streak of stubbornness. As it is at home there is no compromise. I seem prepared to put everything on the line, including my marriage. Heather, despite my pleading, will not support me in this fight. My mother will not talk about it. Maybe if I understood myself — maybe then.

Curly and Lawrence will be in my corner. I'm training in Parrsboro Monday and Friday, in Moncton the rest of the week. As the fight nears and fishing falls off, I start at six in the morning and go until late afternoon. The opponents he gives me get better every week, that's the way Leo wants it. I give the guy credit. It's working.

176

My timing is getting to the point my combinations roll off my shoulders, right, left, right, left. Sharp jabs, not glancing blows but hard solid punches that vibrate up your arms, letting you know you've come in contact with something hard.

Friday night, at the end of my fifth week, I leave word for Leo I won't be in tomorrow. I need an extra day of rest. I can spend the day with Ginny, giving Mabel and my mother a break. It's right after lunch Saturday when Leo shows up. His appearance sends Heather upstairs to my mother's kitchen.

"I'm sorry you decided not to work today. I had some newspaper guys comin' in to watch you. Could have been good publicity." He refuses coffee and is clearly angry. "It's hard not having you in Moncton all the time. Any chance you can come up tonight, take a couple of hours for some photographs for the papers Monday? I told the guys that drinks will be on me if they drop by tonight with their cameras. What d'ya say?"

"I don't think so, Leo. I've been putting in long hours and it's best I rest a couple of days. Besides, I've got plans with Ginny this afternoon. Let's do it Monday."

"We only got four weeks left, Duff. I need all the photos I can get. This is important."

"Give it a break, Leo. The fight is going to be sold out."

Leo isn't taking no for an answer. He gets pushy and is making me mad but at the same time, he's kind of funny. He starts in on how much he has riding on this fight, the money he's put into my training, the promotion. He even pays for my gas back and forth to Moncton.

"The least you can do is cooperate," he shouts in that whiney, irritating voice of his.

"Mr. Cormier." It's almost a shriek and down the stairs my mother flies. She comes into the room with storm clouds in her eyes. It's the look that always made the old man back off, but Leo isn't that smart. He starts to argue with her. The two of them are going toe to toe. I can't help but think of the old man, knowing he'd be smirking if he could see this. My mother isn't giving an inch.

"Duff is putting everything he has into this fight. You should be glad to have someone who is so prepared and all you do is drive down here and hound him about pictures and reporters you've ar-

177

ranged without telling him in advance! You have no consideration. No! He will not go up tonight nor tomorrow, and that's that."

I suppose it's embarrassing having your mother coming to your defense, but the entire exchange is so funny I can't get upset. However, neither of them sees anything amusing. In fact, Leo is getting so angry I become the ref before my mother nails him with a left hook.

"All right, all right, that's enough." I say. "Leo, stop badgering my mother. I'm not going to Moncton today or tomorrow and I'm not wild about you coming into my home, trying to drag me out. You've got no beef with me. I'm training hard, and I've got sense enough to know when to rest. You don't know when to back off." I give him my best evil eye, the Boris Karloff imitation I used to practice in front of the bathroom mirror. "So, Leo, back off right now!"

He mumbles a weak apology while looking at the floor, and leaves.

My mother and I stare at each other, waiting to see who will speak first. Once, when I was very small, a man tried to grab my mother's purse by Douglas' Hardware store in Amherst. He ran past her and tried to yank it off her shoulder. The strap didn't break and she didn't let go. She planted her feet firmly on the ground, held onto the strap with one hand, never letting go of me with the other. Then, at the top of her voice, she quoted Emily Brontë.

"No coward soul is mine,
No trembler in the world's storm-troubled sphere,
I see Heaven's glories shine,
And faith shines equal, arming me from fear."

Her voice boomed up and down the street. The guy was drunk and startled by her resistance and the words coming out of her. He gasped, his mouth slack-jawed, his eyes wide with fright. He let go and stumbled away, almost tripping himself in his haste. Years later, she called it her Brontë defense. I wonder if Leo would have fled faster had he faced "No coward soul is mine."

She smiles wistfully, knowing she's overstepped her bounds. Wondering perhaps, where our relationship is at this moment.

"I never liked that man from the first moment I saw him."

"Is that right, Rocky?" I say, doing the bob and weave around her.

36

GINNY

Her tiny feet can't stay out of the stream as we practice the fine art of catching brookies, the small speckled trout found in the brooks of the Cobequids. Ginny has a face covered with freckles. Her white hair is like corn silk and she is tall for her age. She is also very inquisitive and fishing only holds her attention as long as the brookies are biting. Out of nowhere she can fire a question at me. With a growing vocabulary built on the books my mother constantly reads to her, she can frame more difficult questions and express greater disappointment with my answers.

"If those cows eat green grass, how come their milk is white?"

"I don't know."

"How come you never know?"

"How come you ask so many questions?"

At times, frustrated with her pestering, I snap at her, saying she has to accept the fact I don't know the answer to everything. One day she mulls over such a reply as we walk along a woods trail. After a few seconds, she says in her best haughty voice, "Fine then. I'll ask Uncle Curly." She watches, first confused, then delighted she has made me laugh.

"You just go right ahead."

At other times she is restless for answers. Sitting on a log at the edge of a large blueberry field, she asks me again about the day she went overboard. Her only vivid recollection is one of fear and cold. She challenges me in ways I've never been challenged in the ring. Sometimes I can't hide the pain this event has caused us. Heather sometimes joins us walking in the woods. The smooth sound of brooks and birds puts Ginny to sleep. I suddenly have my wife away from any distractions.

"I want you to know," I begin, "I'll never go back in the ring." I take a deep breath and say the sentence that almost kills me. "I'll sell the boat and quit fishing."

She looks at me, a sad lonely look. We're sitting on old tree stumps, facing each other. "I'm leaving you, Duff. I'm sorry. But," she looks away, "I'm going back to nursing. I can't take Ginny. I know it would kill your mother and besides, I have to finish my training. It breaks my heart to leave her, but I can't stay with you."

There is silence. All I can hear is the wind whistling through the trees. I'm numb, can't say or even think of anything. How does one react to this? Finally, the best I can muster is to ask a question, the answer to which I already fear.

"You wouldn't really leave me. Leave us?"

She sobs, gets up, touches Gin's hair and leaves us there.

Later that evening, a teary-faced Mabel is at my mother's door. Since our wedding, they have become close, joined by a granddaughter bond. Mabel is a hard-working woman who left school early to help support her many brothers and sisters. She smokes, likes a drink of dark rum and plays canasta. My mother might have a glass of wine at Christmas. She is a non-smoker and plays a powerful game of bridge. Lawrence says Mabel has never read a book and my mother reads them all. Ginny is their only granddaughter. That's why Mabel is at my mother's door at ten o'clock at night. Heather has told her. In the light of the forty-watt bulb on the front porch, I can look up from my basement apartment and see she's been crying. During the past four hours, while Ginny slept, I've walked around the apartment like a dead man. I'm glad she's still asleep because I'm in no condition to look after her.

Mabel stays a long time. It's past midnight when she leaves. Heather hasn't come back. When Mabel's car, a gray Austin, pulls out of our driveway, my mother comes down the stairs. She is ashen-faced and shaky.

"Stop her."

"I don't want to talk about it."

"Duff, don't let her go."

Then she says something she shouldn't. "What will people say?" She knows immediately it's a mistake. "God, she's going to leave that lovely girl."

Early the next morning I drive down to Mabel's. Heather doesn't look like she's had any more sleep than me. We walk outside, through the backyard and down the small bank to the beach.

"I want to get some of my things and say good-bye to Ginny. I'm going right away but I'll be back."

"Back to us?" I ask.

"Back to Ginny."

"And me, Heather, what about me?"

"It's not that I don't love you, Duff. Even though you've broken a promise to me, I'm entrusting you with the most precious thing I have. I'm leaving Ginny with you. And it's not that you're not a good man. But — " She pauses and looks me directly in the eye. "All right, hear it. You're just not the man for me."

I feel my face flush. She continues to talk and I hear her, but my mind is somewhere else. It's in the dressing room in Philadelphia and George Bryson is telling me I'm not good enough. So different from hearing all your life that you're the best. I hear Heather through a haze.

"I need someone who isn't so driven."

"I told you," I interrupt, "I'll give up the sea and I swear to God, Heather, I'll never step in the ring again."

"But even if that were true, you'd still be you. Alex Martin would still be in there, pushing you around. You think you're free of your father because he's dead. I live with my father everyday, even though I haven't seen him since I was fourteen."

"Maybe it's time we put both our fathers behind us," I blurt.

She gives me a weary smile full of pain and takes my hand. "Do you know what it means to leave my daughter? My mother is heart-broken and so is yours. I hate the misery I'm causing them. I wouldn't do this if I didn't have to. But Duff, I do have to."

181

She turns away again.

"I know we're going to face a lot of gossip from people. You'll be here, having to face it everyday, people whispering behind your back, pointing at you, saying there's the man whose wife left him. But who can handle it better than you? I've always been intimidated by your courage. Now I'm glad you have it. Since I saw my daughter go over the side of that boat, I've dug deeper into myself than I ever thought I could. I've finally got the courage to tell you the truth, Duff Martin. I married the wrong man."

She kisses me lightly and walks away. I have no defense because I know she is right.

At first, Ginny doesn't grasp her mother's leaving.

"Mummy's going back to her training" is the way we put it. "She's going to be a nurse."

"So she can look after me if I get sick?"

"Yes, dear. So she can look after you."

I carry her around in my arms every evening and I train like hell everyday. Around the four-mile square the voices compete with each other. Bryson, Heather, Ginny, my old man.

Outside of town, the Long Hill diner makes the best hamburgers in Cumberland County. Ginny and I drive up one Sunday afternoon two weeks after Heather has left. Sitting at the counter, she swings her legs and munches a burger with total contentment. As quickly as she can devour a french fry, she can unleash a flurry of inquiries. Where does water come from? How come birds can't fly upside down? Then finishing her burger, she looks at me.

"Daddy, are you going to hurt that man?"

"What man?"

"The man you're going to fight. Are you going to hurt him?"

"No."

"Well, Uncle Curly says you'll beat the living snot out of him."

"Ginny!"

"Well, he said it."

"I'll be talking to Uncle Curly about what he says to you."

That evening we climb the steep steps to the bell tower of the United Church so we can look down on Main Street. Maybe I need a new perspective on life or maybe I just want to occupy myself every minute.

"Look at all the roofs," she says. The tide is high and the thin finger of the sea surrounds the pylons of the old wharves behind Main Street, where ships used to load coal and lumber for far off places.

"The cars and people are tiny," Ginny says, peeping through the slats of the bell tower. "Why do people look so tiny? Would Uncle Lawrence look tiny?" At six-two, Lawrence looks like a giant to Ginny but I tell her yes, even Uncle Lawrence would look tiny from up here.

"Uncle Curly would look teeny tiny."

"Yes, he would."

She pricks me with unexpected pain. "I wish Mummy could see this."

"Yes, that would be nice."

Ginny's got some of the old man's contrary streak. She can fall asleep on my shoulder walking in the woods but she never wants to go to bed.

"I'm afraid."

"There is nothing to be afraid of," I assure her.

"Yeah, but you don't know."

"A handful" is the way my mother describes her. Yet Ginny walks in a room and my mother's eyes light up.

It's only a ten minute stroll to Main Street from our house in Whitehall and sometimes we walk past the post office, the two dozen stores, the three restaurants and the movie theatre that make up Main Street. This is the heart of the town. It's here things happen. It's where the band holds Sunday night concerts, where they have Old Home Week parades. When a Black Widow spider was found in a box of bananas at Lavers grocery store, it was displayed on Main Street, right in the store. You could go in and watch it for nothing. When television first came to town, it came to Main Street. People would gather at Roger MacAloney's service station to witness this radio with pictures. The pictures were snowy, and much of the time there was only a test pattern — the profile of an Indian. However, some evenings the reception got better and we stood there in fascination watching Jack Benny or *Our Miss Brooks*. As we make our way up Main Street to see Gene Autry in the Saturday matinee at the Gem theatre, men with droopy hats and tattooed arms sit on the front steps of some of the stores, smoking. Ginny always looks them over and always asks, "What are they doing?"

I always answer, "Sitting."

She casts one look back as we pass, flicking her white hair over her shoulders. "Oh," she says.

It's a sleepy little town, whose heyday left with the wooden ships, but to Ginny, it's a place full of wonder and adventure. To me it's home and a good place to be.

The next weekend, Dewey comes home from university. He wants to talk about Heather.

"No, Dew. I don't want to talk about her."

There is silence. "I saw her, Duff, this week."

"Where?"

"In Halifax. Walking along Spring Garden Road."

There is something wrong, something in his voice. "Who was she with, Dew?"

"Danny."

I leave him sitting on my front steps and don't stop until I'm at Mabel's front door.

There is a look of alarm in her eyes.

"Mabel, did you know? Did you know she was seeing Danny?"

"Duff." She backs up slightly. "Danny drops by and they go out sometimes for a pop or something. She's very miserable. Danny is some company."

I don't believe her. She's lying through her teeth and my fists are clenched when I walk back into my driveway. Dewey is still sitting there, as if he knew where I was going and that I'd be back.

For the next several hours I spew out my hostility.

"You could go to her."

"No, I'm not going to her!"

"If you wait for her to come back, she may not come."

"Let's get the keys from Curly and go up to the club. I want to work on the bag."

It's several weeks before I can continue to mull over business prospects. There is an old boathouse in Whitehall, not far from my place.

"It's been empty for years," Lawrence says. "Maybe you should see about buying it."

184

"After the fight, maybe I'll do just that."

Things remain cool between Leo and me. He and his brother still gives me pointers but there is a chill in the air. Heading for Parrsboro after a day's training in the Moncton gym, I give Leo a drive to his sister's house and he sees a book on boat building in my car. When I tell him my idea, he says he can help.

"A guy I grew up with, George Leblanc, he's been building Cape Islanders for twenty years."

George is a white-haired, barrel-chested man of boundless energy. He looks like an aging wrestler, one who hasn't totally lost his physique. He's also a sports nut and boxing helps open the door. George gives me the goods on boat building. His boat yard is in Shediac, outside of Moncton, and I start dropping in to see him on my way home.

"Building boats is like any other thing connected to the sea. You make a little money one year and lose it the next. Just don't expect to get rich."

His brown, weather-beaten face breaks into a smile.

The next day in Parrsboro the bank manager and I inspect the empty boat shed. He's doubtful.

"You've never built a boat, Duff. Do you have anyone who can help you get started?"

"Yes. If he'll come."

Curly isn't impressed with boat building. He's upset Kid Carter is calling me names again. He's using words like Dogpatch in interviews with the newspapers. Carter grew up in Ottawa and fights out of Montreal, civilized places, he says. The day he calls Parrsboro Dogpatch, I accidentally crack the ribs of one of my sparring partners in Moncton. The guy's name is Raymond and he's in anguish. Leo takes him to the hospital. The gym is full of fighters, regulars, a few reporters and visitors, so the story spreads that I'm half killing sparring partners. It gets in the newspapers too and there are no more statements from Kid Carter. The fight is a week away. Lawrence and Curly will fly with me out of Moncton with Arlie and Leo.

"Here comes Dogpatch," laughs Lawrence.

He isn't bothered by anything but high-strung Curly is in a flap. What to take, what to wear, should he take two pair of shoes?

"I didn't know you had two pair of shoes," Lawrence says.

A serious Curly answers, "Well, I mean one pair of shoes and a pair of sneakers."

"You'll be a fashion plate, Curly."

Leo supplies custom shirts to Lawrence and Curly. As my cornermen, this time they'll look the part. The shirts warm them up a bit toward Leo, who still didn't want to take them to Montreal and fought it until the final week. Tired of his whining, I finally laid it on the line. "If they don't go, I don't go."

"Goddamn it, Duff!"

"Goddamn it, Leo! Never again will I step in a ring without people I know in my corner. It's that simple."

"Arlie will be there."

"Arlie isn't good enough."

Manny and I are corresponding again. Every couple of weeks I drop him a line about the boathouse, asking his advice. He writes one- or two-page letters in a broad, slanted scrawl. He's having what he calls "a spot of heart trouble, nothing serious. Serves me right for going to a doctor. They're paid to find something wrong."

He tells me Cory has run off with a boat salesman and Mrs. Mac is in tears. I write her too, a long letter telling her everything.

I often take down Manny's spy glass and just hold it, like I did on the bus. Some days I take it down to the beach and look out as far over the water as I can. Everyone in town knows Heather has left me. Probably they know about Danny, too. Yes, I think, of course they do. Through the pain and embarrassment, there is something else nagging me. What I did in Philadelphia. The Jack Johnson photograph. I can see it in the garbage can. I'm sorry about that too.

Music can lift my spirits and it's always a good day when you hear the band. Parrsboro has a citizens band, one of the best around. Sometimes they practice playing and marching around the four-mile square. I like meeting up with them when I'm running. You can hear the music a long way off and it gives a lift to roadwork. I hear them now. It's a beautiful spring day and after a winter cooped up in the band hall they're ready for a little marching drill. I'm running in the opposite direction. When they're in their red uniforms they really stand out. They're harder to spot in street clothes but at a quarter mile the scene comes into perspective. They're marching past a field of grazing cows and strike up "Colonel Bogey." The sudden sound startles the cows, and the frightened animals, so passive one minute, come to life. Three of them crash into the old wooden fence, giving it such a jolt the railings give way and the cows bolt for freedom. They're confused by the direction of the music and instead of running away from the band make right for it. Over the bars of "Colonel Bogey" the bandsmen gaze at the breakaway cattle bearing down on them. There are sour notes, musical miscues and squawks as the bandsmen break rank and run. Suddenly, the road is filled with people and cattle, mooing and laughing. Only Basil the bass drummer continues beating away, keeping time to the chaos.

"That's why we don't invite cows to the concerts," Bernie Burke, the band master, tells me as I pass. "No music appreciation."

I'm doing two trips around the square today and when I return thirty minutes later the band is nowhere to be found. The cattle are peacefully grazing on both sides of Western Avenue near the broken fence. The road is covered with cowshit. Yes, despite the pain I've been handed lately, I do love Parrsboro.

37

MONTREAL

Curly was in France during the war. He's been up to Montreal to see Frankie Henwood fight, so we don't know what accounts for him being the world's most fidgety traveler. I can't sit beside him. He's jumping up and down, squirming, scratching and twitching and we're only going to the airport.

"When we get on the plane, sit by the window, Lawrence, please," Curly says. "I don't like it."

"Nobody's fallen out this week," Lawrence says and doesn't crack a smile.

Leo isn't smiling either. When we meet him inside the Moncton airport, he's holding a newspaper.

"Did you see this?" He hands me a copy of the Fredericton *Gleaner*. It's turned to the sports page with a picture of Kid Carter and the headline "Carter Predicts Victory in Five."

"He's trying to needle you," Curly says. "Figures if he makes you mad you'll carry it into the ring."

Sometimes Curly sounds exactly like the old man. Leo just gives him a hard look.

"Duff," Leo says. "I don't know anyone with your ring smarts. This guy is trying everything. He's cagey and a veteran, don't let this stuff get to you."

"Don't worry, Leo, I'm ready."

Leo loosens up and smiles.

"Your father taught you well."

"Alex Martin knew more about boxing than the rest of us put together," Curly blurts out. Leo frowns again. Curly just won't give Leo respect.

On the plane Curly sits across the aisle from me.

"Promise me something, Duff, when you win. This time you won't quit like that. Like you did last time, so fast."

"I promise, Curly. This time I won't quit so fast. If I win this time, I'll give us all a chance to enjoy it." I realize, much as I want it over, that deep inside, this business of boxing isn't finished.

After checking into our hotel, the three of us walk down Saint Catherine's Street. Lawrence, in his red and black checkered jacket, looks in every store window. It takes half an hour to go one block.

"I didn't know you was such a window shopper, Lawrence."

"A what?"

"A window shopper. You know, someone who stares in store windows."

"Oh."

Montreal is a place Heather and I often talked of going. A second honeymoon some day.

"Think tomorrow I'll get up early and run."

Curly shrugs. "Maybe you should kind of take it easy, Duff."

At six in the morning I'm running the downtown streets. The sidewalks are wet and there is the smell of coffee and gasoline and the noise of trucks unloading, as the city prepares for another day. At the base of Mount Royal I run up the hill, higher and higher I go, overlooking the city. It's up here, as I pass the fancy houses of Montreal's well-to-do, I hear his voice for the first time in months. It's a simple declarative statement. "Kid Carter has had his best years in boxing. Yours are yet to come."

At an afternoon news conference, what Leo calls the last big push to promote the fight, I sit down next to Kid Carter. He doesn't look at me. We shake hands for the cameras but he doesn't make eye contact. I want him to.

We're at a long table in front of the press. Kid Carter's manager and Leo do most of the talking. When a reporter asks me about my chances against Carter, it comes out of me, word for word.

"Kid Carter has had his best years in boxing. Mine are yet to come."

I say the words loudly, clearly and the room goes quiet. Curly and Lawrence are in the front row. Curly looks proudly at me. Lawrence has that small knowing grin. Carter just snorts but I have the room in my hand and I press my advantage.

"I beat him when he was younger and I'll beat him again."

I smile, look at Curly and tell the room, "I'm ready."

38

WE'RE EVEN

Every fight I've ever had is going through me now — Juan, Snooky, Jack Ryan, I see them all as Curly ties my gloves. The Montreal Forum is packed, hot and noisy. Seven fights on the card. We are the sixth. Even a Canadian middleweight championship doesn't get top billing here. Leo explains.

"The organizers don't trust you. You could go down in the first round and they want a big fight at the top of the card." He says he tried hard for top spot but they wouldn't budge.

"Not with a fighter who doesn't fight, who doesn't have a track record."

Two ranking world heavyweights are the main event. Fine with me. I came here to fight. Few give me a chance and much of what's been written isn't flattering. Kid Carter is fighting a Nova Scotia nobody who knocked him out a couple of years back. It's what they call a curiosity fight and the reporting sounds much like it did the first time. The *Montreal Gazette* puts it this way:

"If our young Nova Scotia friend wins tonight, he'll be the first champion in the history of Canadian boxing who had only two fights in his division. How farcical can boxing get?" The French papers say Carter is out of his mind and leave it at that.

So here we go down the aisle, me in the middle, Lawrence on my left, Curly on my right. Three guys from Parrsboro in the big time. Security people all around us. The usual boos and catcalls coming out of the smoke. I follow the old man's rules. Don't look at the crowd, stay loose, rest the day of the fight except for the legs. Give the legs a workout. Above all, keep the mind clear of everything but the fight. Study your opponent and change your stance, never let him set the pace.

Kid Carter gets an overwhelming ovation. People stand and cheer.

"They'll be cheering out of the other side of their face when we're through with them," says Curly. Lawrence nods. A cloud of smoke hangs over the ring. The noise is deafening. Flashbulbs pop.

I'm inside myself, listening to his raspy voice. "Listen, kid, he's going to be aggressive. He's going to carry the fight to you."

Kid Carter still doesn't look at me during the ref's instructions. I never take my eyes off him. Finally, when we touch gloves he looks at me and I scream as loudly as I can, "Dogpatch!"

He hears me over the noise; a faint smile comes to the corners of his mouth.

"What did you say?" asks Lawrence.

"Dogpatch. I said Dogpatch."

"Why?" asks Lawrence.

"Because that's where I'm going to send him."

"Yippee!" yells Curly.

The bell rings.

Kid Carter has been Canadian champ almost a decade. He's not going to make sloppy mistakes, so there is no shortcut. This is a grind 'em down fight, a weary wearing away of your opponent. I settle in for a siege.

He hits hard and often. He may be twenty-nine but he can still snap a sharp jab. The leather smacking my face can be heard twenty rows away. My cheeks are burning although I'm snapping some pretty good jabs myself. One advantage I have is my height. He's shorter and I can punch down at him. We test each other, bobbing and weaving. In the first seconds, our faces are already covered in sweat. Carter doesn't waste punches. As a film of sweat quickly covers me, his jabs take on the sound of hot wires crackling. We're in a flurry. Repeated snaps like tiny bullets fly through the air. These are not powerful body blows that bend you over, but sharp hornet stings. Take enough of them and they'll disable you. The bell rings and the crowd explodes. A good round.

"Those jabs, God! You can hear them all over Montreal," Curly says, taking out my mouthpiece.

"He doesn't make many mistakes," I respond.

"Neither do you," says Lawrence.

As the bell sounds for round two I hear the old man say just one word: "Watch."

We're more cautious in round two. We fire fewer jabs and stay farther away. The seconds tick by with both of us circling the ring. The fans get restless easily and the catcalls start: "Come on, hit 'em." The bell rings.

The old man always said never react to the fans. Even so I want to press him in round three.

"I'm going to push him a little," I tell Curly. Lawrence frowns.

"Duff, be careful, he's a tricky son-of-a-bitch."

"Right now you're even. Maybe you should wait a couple," suggests Curly.

"I can't explain it, Curly, but I think it's time to put some heavy hooks on him."

Kid Carter must have the same idea. He immediately puts a hard left hook into me, a slamming blow that breaks my breath. I try to recover with a right into his midsection and a left to his head. The left connects, hurling the sweat off his face in a wet arc that flies across the ring. He misses with a left and I throw another hook. It misses and he backs off. Breathless, I still push him. Two jabs and another hook hit him. He fires an unusually wide haymaker that's so close I can feel the hot air. Whoosh.

The flashbulbs never stop. People smell blood. The crowd is constantly roaring. Carter tags me with jabs, one-two and another one. I hit him with a right cross. The bell rings.

Curly is talking so fast his spittle is flying in all directions.

"You took that round."

"Good round," says Lawrence.

The bell rings and Carter comes at me. He's firing jabs and combinations. My face burns like it's on fire. The old man always told me to do the unexpected. You can't think over choices, you have to feel them in your gut — instinct. Instinct is telling me to keep pushing, to bob into him with a right cross. I do. It knocks him back and for a few short seconds, I have the advantage. I'm on him with a right cross and a hard hook and the crowd is on its feet. Carter gamely battles back. I don't know where his punch comes from but he lands a hook to the side of my face. The impact spins me around. The ref calls time to look at me.

"You all right?"

I've got my mouthpiece in so all I can do is nod. I give him the gloves up sign and the round continues. Carter tags me with another hard jab. The bell ends round four. It's my worst round.

"He's tagging you with that left of his. Keep your guard a little higher and stay away. Remember what Alex always told you about being on your bicycle." Curly is giving instructions and water, Lawrence is toweling me down. There is a little splatter of blood on my arm, like the drop, that day, under the old man's nose.

"Use your legs," someone says to me. Maybe Curly, maybe it's in my head. I'm seven years younger than Carter. I should be floating more, moving in and out, letting him come to me. We fight through rounds five and six. I'm giving it all I've got. He wins five. Six is about even. I've got a cut above my right eye and he keeps hammering at it. I've split his lower lip again, as I did in our first fight, and it bleeds so much the ref halts the fight in round seven to look at it. We're both beaten up. Lawrence and Curly look at me with concern. We don't talk. I wait for round eight. I think of Juan and Philadelphia. Maybe it's my face burning as it was then, when Juan peppered me with his hard punches.

I close my eyes and hear his voice. "It takes grit. All great fighters have grit. It's grit." He talked grit to every new guy in the club. Grit isn't training, isn't talent, it's in you, deep inside you.

I look at my gloves.

Carter is ahead on points and he's up before the bell. We have three rounds left. As we come out of our corners, I take his measure. His lower lip is puffy, his right eye partially closed, a swelling around his right cheek. I'm no better. This fight could be stopped at any moment. Then I hear the old man; he only says it once but it's him, his nasal, distinctive voice.

"Win and we're even."

We'll be even. Even! I smile at Kid Carter and he glares back at me, hostility and hate in his eyes.

We'd be even. Yes, we would.

He's funny, Kid Carter is. His face looks like it's made out of putty and I've just rearranged part of it. Now I'm dancing and laughing. Yes, even. We'll be even.

39

Epiphany

You have to have worn a mouthpiece to understand laughing when wearing one. It's all laughing on the inside. Pure delight is flowing over me. Joy, peace. I'm having — what's the word? — an epiphany. I'm having an epiphany in the eighth round. I'm here, doing it, fighting for the Canadian title and if I win, my debt is paid. Paid, you understand, paid!

The ref is eyeing me. Carter seems confused. He's trying to wipe the smile off my face with a combination of lefts and rights. I walk through them and hit him hard. A right hook shakes him. Then I jab one-two-three; he tries to counterpunch. Then I let it go, the right again, my best punch. This time in full power with my legs anchored to the canvas. It's the punch perfected in our basement. The punch thrown at Snooky and Jack Ryan. The right that knocked Cutter to the canvas in Boston and made the Cubans respect me.

It's the right he taught me over hours of practice, getting the stance, using the legs, following through. It's everything I have. The power coming through me, all the energy in my body channeled into my right hand and it all goes into Kid Carter's face. It is the hardest punch I've ever thrown. I know this because of the pain that shoots up my arm and vibrates down my side.

Carter's head gives a violent jolt and the whiplash launches his mouthpiece across the ring. Only the whites of his eyes are visible as his arms drop to his sides. His knees buckle, his legs crumple. There will be no more from Kid Carter tonight. He is finished.

Pandemonium! People are in the ring working on Carter. Fans jump in and slap me on the back. I can't hear them; the noise is like a violent storm. Curly is crying, big pear-shaped tears rolling down his cheeks. Lawrence just hugs me. Powerful arms picking me up off the canvas and carrying me around the ring. When they put the Canadian Middleweight Championship belt on me, I raise my arms in the air. It's his moment of glory. The old man's got his champ.

At the post fight news conference, some reporters get surly when I won't give them a straight answer about my plans or about a possible rematch. I smile because I really don't care. I'm not throwing away my gloves this time. I don't have to.

"God, those guys were rough on you," Curly says. "Think they'd have more respect for the Canadian champion." He hugs me again.

We go to a wonderful restaurant in Montreal at the top of a big hotel. Leo's treat. He's already talking about a rematch or a possible world title shot. But I know better.

After a few days, the interviews and handshakes are over and I'm back in the boathouse. I paid the back taxes and bought it for a song. It needs plenty of repairs and I work round the clock, fixing the roof, replacing most of the windows and one of the wide doors at the end of the long shed that has broken away from the hinge. I write Manny, asking if there is any way he could come, just as an advisor for a couple of weeks, to oversee the laying of my first keel. He'll come for two weeks, but doesn't want anything but room and board because, in his words, "I can't work like I used to." I send him money for his ticket and thank God that he's agreed.

When he's not fishing, Lawrence gives me a hand. The fight money is going into the business and I know it will be months before a boat is ready to sell. It's taking a lot of time, money and paint but is giving me a sense of satisfaction. Lawrence and Curly are repairing the floor and even George Leblanc has come down to help me with construction plans. George and I both agree, even though I eventually want to build schooners, I should start with Cape Islanders. In the early years they'll be the core of my business but someday schooners

197

and sloops will be built here, employing all the old methods that I can use. It's the kind of boat building that's almost a lost art and it's an art I want to restore. The first sloop I'm going to call the *Ginny & Jean*. The second one will be called the *Martha Jane*.

We're all working away on a Sunday afternoon. The lumber for the first keel is coming next week and we're building new skids when the door opens and in walks . . . my God, it's Mouse. He isn't in uniform but still has that big moon-faced smile.

"Mouse, what are you doing here? We weren't expecting you for a long, long time," says Curly.

"Yeah, I know. Things change. I quit the army." He says it rather sheepishly, much like the expression he used years ago at the Halifax Forum.

"Why?" we all ask at once.

"Ah, shit," he sighs. "It's a long story." Then he leans back on our new workbench, grins and takes out a smoke. "Basically I got thrown in the brig for punching a sergeant, son-of-a-bitch."

"Mouse." I put my hand on his shoulder. It's not that difficult to read Mouse and I know when he's unhappy. I've also come home with my pride diminished.

"Did they kick you out?"

"Nope," he says indignantly, "I quit." Then he shrugs. "I guess they would have. They gave me a choice and I took it. Honorable discharge."

"What are you gonna do now?" Curly asks a little too directly.

"Find a job, I guess. What are you doing, Duff? Mabel says you're going to build boats."

"That's right. Starting next week."

"Need a hand?"

"Mouse, you know even less about boat building than I do. One greenhorn is enough."

"Yeah, well, nothing says I can't learn."

That night Mouse, Lawrence, Curly and I sit on a log watching the tide come in.

"You gonna stick around Parrsboro?" Curly asks Mouse.

"Don't know."

"I can always use a hand in the club."

"Are you helping, Duff?" Mouse asks.

"No, Mouse, I've got my hands full."

"Maybe later he will," Curly says. "I got some good prospects this fall. I can always use another trainer."

"Sure," says Mouse. "All right."

Heather comes back occasional weekends and takes Ginny to her mother's house. Today she told me she wants a divorce. I didn't argue. I don't anymore. Lawrence is home with his wife. Curly, Mouse and I are sitting on the beach watching the sun go down. Curly has a pint of dark rum and he and Mouse are sipping from the bottle. I didn't want any. They're drinking and I'm looking. I raise Manny's spy glass. Across the Minas Basin, the lights near Hantsport twinkle. If I didn't know better, I'd think they were from a ship way off in the distance. I look a long time. The tide laps up the beach, closer and closer to our feet.

40

N ᴇᴡ Hᴏᴘᴇ

The old boathouse is transformed. It has a new coat of paint, a sign I paid way too much for, and a lot of my sweat over the entire building. Between hammering, painting and planning, I had a lot of help. George donated Cape Islander plans and helped me pick a sloop design. He's also spent a lot of time teaching me about selling.

"Building is only half it," he says. "You have to sell them. So the better you prepare to sell, the more effective you'll be."

We collect addresses of yachting magazines and New England newspapers and fishery publications where he suggests I place advertisements — when I'm ready.

My boat business opens the end of August. Dewey is going into his final year of law school and has been working out west this summer, but at my urging he comes home early. I have him stand next to me when I cut the ribbon. The *Parrsboro Record* snaps a photograph. After the ribbon cutting we have coffee and donuts. Half the town shows up to look at the photographs and designs of the Cape Islanders and our sloops. The Martin Boat Building Co. is now in business. Colin Atkinson will give me a hand. Manny gets here next week and George says he's only ninety minutes away.

I hope Heather will show up for the opening but I'm hardly surprised when she doesn't. Leo arrives and no sooner is the ribbon cut than he starts about me defending my title or looking for a big fight in the States. I know better. The next day I write two letters, one to the Canadian Boxing Association, the other one to Leo. They both say the same thing — "I quit."

The boathouse keeps me very preoccupied. Mouse is working for me, as I knew he would. He can work hard and is pretty good with his hands. In our first weeks we get a nibble. It's not a firm order, but a Halifax man has been back three times. He wants to buy a Cape Islander with his brother. There have been other inquiries as well, and the bank manager is surprised by the interest. I'm just thankful.

During the summer months old friends home for vacation would drop in to the boathouse to say hello. With autumn, they've gone. Only Lois Tupper is still home. Her husband is on some course at Dalhousie University in Halifax and she spends a lot of time in Parrsboro with her parents. So it's not too surprising when she walks in one Friday while we're working on the keel. Lois always had a flare for the dramatic.

"Duff," she says in a rather coy voice. "You remember Vivien?"

Standing there is Vivien Schuster. I'm dumbstruck! Just as I was that afternoon at Jeffers Falls. With that same self-assured manner I've always found so appealing, Vivien walks right up to me. "Hello, Duff."

"Vivien, what . . . what are you doing here?" Mouse stops to watch.

"Just visiting. I haven't been here since — " she pauses. "Ah, since the . . . ah . . . summer, that summer."

It's my turn for self-assurance. I take her shoulders and kiss her on the cheek, not a peck but a kiss, a long soft kiss. Lois looks away. Mouse clears his throat and takes a drink of water.

"I know exactly what summer you mean." She puts her arms around me and a sensation comes over me. I feel, what is it? Yes, warmth. I feel warmth.

"How long will you be here?"

"I don't know. I got my teaching degree a year ago and guess what?" She draws away and laughs, "I'm not cut out to be a teacher.

Isn't that rich?" She smiles and takes a breath. "Things are up in the air. I don't know, maybe a couple of weeks."

We walk to the beach. She squeezes my hand and a thousand electric currents go through me.

"How are you really, Duff?"

"I'm fine, Vivien. You know, a lot has happened to me."

"I keep up with your life as best I can. I know you're the Canadian middleweight champ and I know you have a daughter."

"I'm sure you know other things as well."

"I'm sorry, Duff. It must be very hard."

Those beautiful eyes, she doesn't let on I'm staring at her.

"I'd like you to meet my daughter."

"You would?"

"Yes."

Over the next few days we have dinner on the beach and take Ginny down the shore to Advocate Harbour. We talk as Ginny chases seagulls in the surf. I tell her about my father's death, about Heather and our marriage, of my happiness and depression. She tells me about her life in college and the gradual realization that both the man she was engaged to and her chosen career were wrong for her.

"I haven't found my calling yet."

"Finding your calling is really finding yourself."

"How do you do that?" she asks.

"All I know is it's a struggle. A struggle within yourself."

"So is giving up a career you set your heart on, that you built your dreams on."

"What happened?" I ask.

"I love children but I found the school system stifling. There was so much politics. It just didn't suit me."

Her talent with children is apparent. There is none of the reserve Ginny has for most people. "Do you like my daddy?" she asks Vivien candidly.

"Yes, I do and I like you too."

"Do you like my mummy?"

"I don't know your mummy but I bet she's very nice."

"She is, but she doesn't live with us. Only she comes some weekends and takes me with her."

With that Ginny runs down the beach.

"She seems to take things well," Vivien says.

"Not so well as you might think. A lot of nights she calls for her mother."

"Oh, Duff. You're doing so well with her and with yourself."

"Vivien, let's go back to Jeffers Falls, remember?"

She smiles at me. "Why?"

"I don't know, let's just do it."

A couple of days later, we take a bottle of wine and sit on the rocks by the pool at the bottom of the falls. It's one of those afternoons that Mother Nature made for talking. I've been opening up to her but today everything comes out of me. How I poured my life into fishing, then boxing and now boat building.

"Are you running from something?" she asks.

"Maybe."

"Maybe from yourself."

"Maybe."

"I would love to have your passion, Duff. To go into things the way you do. Would you teach me to sail?"

"You? You want to sail?"

"Why not? I remember being on your catboat. I remember calling you Captain Bligh and you kissing me."

"I kissed you a lot."

"You certainly did."

The next day I surprise Mouse by telling him I'm taking a few afternoons off. "When the tide is right," I add.

"You goin' fishin'?"

"Sailing."

By our fourth afternoon on the water, she handles the little catboat like a pro. We anchor near Fox Point for a picnic lunch. That's when I ask her.

"Stay, please."

"Stay here?"

"Yes, here with me."

She leans over and touches my face. Heat runs through me like an electric current.

"Stay, Viv, please. I know I'm asking a lot, but . . . "

"Duff, if you want me to stay, I'll stay for as long as you want me to. But right now I'm turning this boat around. I want to tie up at the wharf and I want to go back to the falls."

"Now?" I ask.

"Yes, right now, I want you to ask me to stay again. There."

In the late afternoon sun we walk above the falls and make love in the long grass. What flows out of me takes with it all the tension and heartache of a lifetime. We lay in each other's arms, listening to the birds and looking at the sky. White, fluffy clouds drift by. One looks like Snooky Redden, another resembles the *Martha Jane*. Then a host of sailing ships, a fluffy armada crossing the sky. It is getting dark when Vivien wakes me. The clouds are now almost still, dressed in silver trim supplied by an autumn moon. We walk hand-in-hand down the moonlit hill to my car.

The next afternoon we leave for the Oxford Exhibition. An excited Ginny is being contained by my mother in the back seat. Vivien sits close to me. On our way out of town, we pass the boxing club. Curly is just unlocking the door for Saturday practice. He turns on the lights and just for an instant I see an image, a passing flicker of a limping man with tussled hair. Vivien looks up at me when I say softly, "We're even."

Epilogue

1985

The spinnaker flaps a few times and firmly catches the breeze, the last of the sails to be unfurled. We've lengthened the masts on this schooner and made the bowsprit longer. As a counterbalance the keel is deeper. She draws more water but can take more canvas. In the first good wind, I know the changes work by the way she cuts the water and the feel of sheer power in my hands. It makes me recall that verse written, years ago, when King George V died.

A sailor he, who knew the joy of tiller feel,
Of listing mast and trembling keel.

I named this schooner the *Northern Enterprise*. Many of the names we use are after ships built along the Parrsboro shore. The original *Northern Enterprise* was actually built in Economy over a century ago. A fine ship then and a fine ship now.

I'm alone today and will have another week to put the schooner through its paces before the buyer arrives from New Jersey. Dr. Gibson and his mates will spend a further week with me and, if satisfied, the doctor will make the final payment and sail away. I'll go with them only as far as Yarmouth, then they're on their own.

Under full sail there is always a sense of freedom. It's been a glorious summer. Ginny and the kids stayed an extra week and Lawrence and his family were home for a while. We sailed almost every day. Those twins of Ginny's show real sailing ability, especially Mark, who loves the water as much as his mother.

Cape Blomidon is directly off my port, the massive headland jutting out of the silvery water like the profile of a stony face. Dr. Gibson knows these waters. He was here five years ago when Bradley Whitelaw purchased his yacht. They spent many days and nights sailing up and down the basin. Gibson and I have kept in touch, more so in the last year since he ordered his own schooner. This will be easy and pleasant, unlike three years ago when a customer who purchased a schooner didn't know the first thing about sailing. He could not begin to handle the ship and I couldn't let it go into his reckless and inexperienced hands. I feared for his life, the life of his crew and that beautiful ship I'd spent months building. I tried to teach that stubborn man and finally refused to sell to him. Over his curses and threats I gave him his money back. Never sold that schooner and never regretted it. Dr. Gibson knows how to sail, has been second in command on Bradley's schooner, from here to Jersey and twice down to Hog's Head and Hatteras.

The wind surges again, sending small vibrations through the wheel and into my hands. The *Northern Enterprise* cuts into the brine. Feel the surge. God, what a lovely craft! Sixty-four feet of graceful power. The air is hot and salty. There can be nothing better. Looking back, my little town is lost in the distance. Only the lighthouse is still visible and getting smaller by the second. I hate the new lighthouse. Small and automated, a saltbox designed by bureacrats without style or taste. Maybe it's age and maybe I live too much in the past. I'm still not used to Main Street, since the big fire during the sixties wiped out Wheaton's, the drug store and the taxi stand. The post office has been closed and replaced with another box-type building similar to the lighthouse. Like the old ships, old buildings slowly disappear. Thank God, many of the captains' big houses still stand as regal testaments to their masters.

There are new things that are good. They've built a seniors' home off King Street. Lawrence and I worked to get Curly into it. Now partially crippled with arthritis, Curly still likes to come down to the boathouse, sit on a stack of lumber and have a beer. He is totally bald.

"The last thing in our youth," Dewey once said, "was Curly's comb-over, and it's disappeared."

Something else is new. Before Ginny and the children went back to Toronto, I took the family to Parrsboro's new theater, on the deck of an old ferry that used to ply the waters of Minas Basin. They all enjoyed the play, a true story about a ship called *Mary Celeste*. She was found floating with the table set for a meal, the cargo, all valuables and provisions intact but not a soul on board — and not a soul ever heard of again. The boys had talked about nothing else for the rest of the evening. I'll take Dr. Gibson and his friends there, give them a clam bake on the beach and maybe half a day of flounder fishing.

As he does with every customer, Mouse wil take them to Advocate Harbour and along the trail to Apple River. Mouse has his stories down pat, including how they used to race horses on Main Street in the old days, where the ships used to tie up, where the Springhill coal was loaded and what former prime minister built the Ottawa House. But most of a buyer's time is spent on the water learning his new vessel, its quirks, strengths and how it handles when the wind suddenly turns into the northeast with bite in its breath.

But now it's my time, alone with the ship, putting it through its paces. I'll stay by their side until they're comfortable and confident in their purchase. We try to make them just as comfortable on land. Vivien and I will prepare dinner for them and she'll hand out autographed copies of her latest children's book to take back to nephews, nieces or grandchildren in the States.

My own children are in far-flung places and much on my mind today. Ginny is the closest. Lawrence is an economics major in England. Manny, my restless nineteen-year-old, is roaming around Africa somewhere. Manny is most like me, I suppose. He can certainly handle a schooner. He told his mother once he spent so much time in the boatyard that the smell had penetrated his pores, giving him a permanent odor of wood shavings. I hope against hope Manny will take over the business. I've put a lot into it and want it to outlast me. There were bleak years, God knows. Markets tumbled and contracts were cancelled. Generally the business grew because I forced it to grow, with several extensions to the boathouse.

When the children were small, I'd carry them around on my shoulders, first Ginny, then Lawrence and finally Manny. They often came down with Vivien to inspect a schooner slowly taking shape. It was Manny who particularly loved the corner office. As a child he found it a fascinating place, cluttered with plans and pictures of various schooners we had built.

The *Northern Enterprise* drives into the water, every sail rigid, every line taut. Yes, Manny will come back. He won't roam forever. I wonder if these thoughts about the family have anything to do with this morning in the boathouse. I'd just been doing some paperwork and felt something, like a pair of eyes on me. I actually stopped what I was doing and looked at the photographs on the wall, really looked at them, got up and closely studied every aspect of every schooner we'd ever built. They were, in a way, part of me and part of my family. I didn't stop at the ships. I studied the last photograph too. The two men — one in a sailor's uniform, smiling, and a bigger man, the black man. A boxer and world champ. Not smiling, but with an expression of loss and sadness in his eyes, standing next to the beaming sailor. It had been a long time, years in fact, since I really looked into the face of my father and Joe Louis. Strange. Who in the world do I understand better than both of them?